"Oh, will she have to stay there forever?"
asked Freddie.

The Bobbsey Twins at Home

BY

LAURA LEE HOPE

AUTHOR OF "THE BOBBSEY TWINS,"

NEW YORK

GROSSET & DUNLAP

PUBLISHERS

Printed in the United States of America

CONTENTS

THE BOBBSEY TWINS
AT HOME

CHAPTER I

TOMMY TODD'S STORY

"MOTHER, how many more stations before
we'll be home?"

"Oh, quite a number, dear. Sit back and
rest yourself. I thought you liked it on the
train."

"I do; but it's so long to sit still."

The little fellow who had asked the question
turned to his golden-haired sister, who sat in
the seat with him.

"Aren't you tired, Flossie?" he asked.

"Yes, Freddie, I am!" exclaimed Flossie.
"And I want a drink of water."

"Dinah will get it for you," said Mother
Bobbsey. "My! But you are a thirsty little
girl."

"Deed an' dat's whut she am!" exclaimed a

1

fat, good-natured looking colored woman, smiling at the little girl. Dinah was the Bobbsey family cook. She had been with them so long that she used to say, and almost do, just what she pleased. "Dis am de forty-sixteen time I'se done bin down to de end ob de car gittin' Miss Flossie a drink ob watah. An' de train rocks so, laik a cradle, dat I done most upsot ebery time. But I'll git you annuder cup ob watah, Flossie lamb!"

"And if you're going to upset, and fall down, Dinah, please do it where we can see you," begged Freddie. "Nothing has happened since we got on this train. Do upset, Dinah!"

"Yes, I want to see it, too," added Flossie. "Here, Freddie, you can have my place at the window, and I'll take yours on the outside. Then I can see Dinah better when the car upsets her."

"No, I want to sit here myself, Flossie. You wanted the window side, and now you must stay there."

"No, I don't want to. I want to see Dinah upset in the aisle. Mamma, make Freddie let me sit where I can see Dinah fall."

"Well, ob all t'ings!" gasped the fat, colored cook. "If you chilluns t'ink dat I'se gwine t' upsot mahse'f so yo' kin see suffin t' laugh at, den all I'se got t' say is I ain't gwine t' do it! No, sah! Not fo' one minute!" And Dinah sat up very straight in her seat.

"Children, be nice now," begged Mother Bobbsey. "I know you are tired with the long ride, but you'll soon hear the brakeman call out 'Lakeport'; and then we'll be home."

"I wish I were home now," said Freddie. "I want to get my dog Snap out of the baggage car, and have some fun with him. I guess he's lonesome for me."

"And he's lonesome for me, too!" cried Flossie. "He's as much my dog as he is yours, Freddie Bobbsey. Isn't he, Mother?"

"Yes, dear, of course. I don't know what's the matter with you two children. You never used to dispute this way."

"I guess the long train ride is tiring them," said Papa Bobbsey, looking up from the paper he was reading.

"Anyhow, half of Snoop, our black cat, is mine then," said Freddie. "Isn't she, Mother?"

"Yes. And now please don't talk like that any more. Look out of the window and watch the trees shoot past."

"Oh, I'm going to see Snoop!" exclaimed Flossie, suddenly.

"So'm I," added Freddie. And in a moment the two children were bending over a basket which was in the seat with Dinah. In the basket was Snoop, the big black cat. She always traveled that way with the Bobbseys. And she seemed very comfortable, for she was curled up on the blanket in the bottom of the basket. Snoop opened her eyes as Freddie and Flossie put their fingers through cracks and stroked her as well as they could.

"I wish Snap was in here with us," said Freddie, after a bit. "I hope he gets a drink of water."

"Oh, I want a drink of water!" exclaimed Flossie, suddenly. "I forgot I was thirsty. Mother, can't I have a drink?" she went on.

"Oh, yes, dear. I suppose so. I'll get it for you."

"No, let Dinah get it so she'll upset," begged Flossie.

"I'll get it for you, Flossie," offered Freddie. "Dinah might get hurt."

"Dat's de li'l gen'man," said the fat cook, smiling. "He lubs ole Dinah."

"I love you too, Dinah," said Flossie, patting the black hand that had done many kind acts for the twins. "But I *do* want a drink, and you know you *would* look funny if you upset here in the car."

"Yes, I spects I would, chile," laughed Dinah.

"May I get Flossie a drink?" asked Freddie.

"You may both go down to the end of the car where the water-cooler is," said Mrs. Bobbsey. "The train is slowing down now, and going to stop, I think, so you won't fail. But be careful."

Flossie and Freddie started toward the end of the long car, but their sister Nan, who with her brother Bert was a few seats away, went with them, to make sure nothing would happen.

"I'm not thirsty any more," Flossie said, after having had two cups of cold water.

"No, but you will be in half an hour, I'm

sure," laughed Nan. "Every one seems to get thirsty on a railroad journey. I do myself," and she took some water after Freddie had had enough.

The train now came to a stop, and Flossie and Freddie hurried back to their seat to look out at the station. Hardly were they both crowded close to the window before there was the sound of shouting and laughing, and into the car came rushing a number of children. With them were two ladies who seemed to be in charge. There were boys and girls—about twenty all together—and most of them made rushes for the best seats, while some hurried down to the tank to get drinks of ice-water.

"I had that cup first!" cried one.

"You did not! I had it myself," said another.

"That's my seat by the window!" shouted a third.

"It is not! I had it first, you can see where I left my hat! Oh, my hat's gone!" a boy exclaimed.

"I threw it on the floor, I wanted to sit here myself," said a big girl with red curls.

"Children! Children! You must be quiet!" called one of the ladies.

The train started again, all the other passengers watching the queer children who were making such a confusion.

"Oh, see the cow!" cried a tall boy. "It's the last cow you'll see for a year, fellows, so take a good look at her," he added as the train passed along a field.

"No more good times for a long while," sighed a boy who had a seat near Freddie and Flossie. "I wish I could live in the country always."

Flossie and Freddie looked at him. His clothes were patched here and there, but they were clean. And his face and hands were clean, which could not be said of all the other children, though some of them showed that they had tried to make themselves neat.

"The country is the best place," he said, and he looked at the two smaller Bobbsey twins as though he would like to speak to them. "I'm going to be a farmer when I grow up," he went on, after a pause.

"He—he's a nice boy," whispered Flossie

to her brother. "I'm going to speak to him. We can talk about the country."

"Wait a minute," advised Freddie. "Maybe mother wouldn't want us to talk to strangers."

Flossie looked back to where her father and mother were sitting. Mrs. Bobbsey was speaking to one of the ladies who had come in the car with the noisy children.

"Are you taking part of an orphan asylum on an outing?" Flossie heard her mother ask.

"No. These are some 'fresh air' children. They have been out in the country for two weeks, and now we are taking them home. Poor things! I wish we could have kept them longer out in the green fields and woods, but there are others waiting for their chance to go.

"You see," she went on, and Flossie and Freddie listened carefully, "some kind people give us money so that the poor children of the city may have a little time in the country during the hot weather. We board them out at different farmers' houses. This company of children has been on two different farms near Branchville, where we just got on the train. Some of the little ones are from Sanderville."

This was a large city not far from Lakeport, a smaller city where the Bobbsey twins lived. "Others are from Lakeport," went on the lady, speaking to Mrs. Bobbsey.

"Indeed!" exclaimed Freddie's mother. "I did not know there was a fresh air society in our city."

"It has only just been formed," said the lady, who was a Miss Carter. "We haven't much money left, I'm sorry to say."

"Then you must let me give you some," said Mr. Bobbsey. "And I will get some friends of mine to give money also. Our own children enjoy it so much in the country that I want to see others have a good time, too."

Then he and Mrs. Bobbsey began to talk about ways of helping poor children, and Flossie and Freddie did not listen any more. Besides, just then the train was passing along a field in which were many horses, some of which raced alongside the cars, and that interested the twins.

"Oh, look at 'em run!" cried the fresh air boy who sat in front of the smaller Bobbsey twins. "Don't they go fast?"

The other fresh air youngsters crowded to their windows to look out, and some tried to push their companions away so they might see better. Then a number all wanted a drink of water at the same time, and the two ladies who were in charge of the children were kept busy making them settle down.

The quiet, neat boy about whom Flossie had whispered to her brother, turned around in his seat and, looking at Freddie, asked:

"Were you ever on a farm?"

"Yes," answered Freddie, "we just came from our uncle Dan's farm, at Meadow Brook. We were there 'most all Summer. Now we're going back home."

"Where do you live, and what's your name?" asked the strange boy.

"My name's Freddie Bobbsey, and this is my sister Flossie," was the answer. "We're twins. Up there, in that other seat, are my brother and sister, Bert and Nan. They're twins too, but they're older'n we are. We live in Lakeport."

"You do?" cried the boy in surprise. "Why, that's where I live! My name is Tommy Todd."

"That's a nice name," put in Flossie politely. "I don't know any one of that name in Lakeport though. Where does your father live?"

Tommy Todd did not answer at once, and Freddie was surprised to see tears in the eyes of the strange boy.

"I—I guess you folks don't ever come down to our part of Lakeport," he said. "We live down near the dumps. It isn't very nice there."

Freddie had heard of the "dumps." It was on the farther side of the city, a long distance from his nice home. Once, when he was very little, he had wandered away and been lost. A policeman who found him had said Freddie was near the "dumps."

Freddie remembered that very well. Afterward, he heard that the "dumps" was a place where the ashes, tin cans, and other things that people threw away were dumped by the scavengers. So Freddie was sure it could not be a very nice place.

"I live out near the dumps, with my grandmother," went on Tommy Todd.

"We've a grandmother too," said Flossie. "We go to see her at Christmas. We've two grandmas. One is my mother's mother, and the other is my father's mother. That's my papa and my mother back there," and Flossie pointed to where Mr. and Mrs. Bobbsey were talking to the fresh air lady.

"Doesn't your father live with you and your grandmother?" asked Freddie.

"I—I haven't any father," said Tommy, and once more the tears came into his eyes. "He was lost at sea. He was a captain on a ship, and it was wrecked."

"Oh, please tell us about it!" begged Freddie. "I just love stories about the ocean; don't you, Flossie?"

"Yes, I do."

"I'm going to be a sea captain when I grow up," said Freddie. "Tell us about your father, Tommy."

So while the train rushed on Tommy Todd told his sad little story.

CHAPTER II

A SUDDEN STOP

"I DON'T remember my father very well," said Tommy Todd. "I was real little when he went away. That was just after my mother died. My grandmother took care of me. I just remember a big man with black hair and whiskers, taking me up in his arms, and kissing me good-bye. That was my father, my grandmother told me afterward."

"What made him go away from you?" asked Flossie. "Didn't he like to stay at home?"

"I guess maybe he did." said Tommy. "But he couldn't stay. He was a sea captain on a ship, you know."

"Of course!" cried Freddie. "Don't you know, Flossie? A sea captain never stays at home, only a little while. He has to go off to steer the ship across the ocean. That's what I'm going to do."

"I don't want you to," returned Flossie, as she nestled up closer to her brother. "I want you to stay with me. If you have to go so far off to be a sea captain couldn't you be something else and stay at home? Couldn't you be a trolley-car conductor?"

"Well, maybe I could," said Freddie slowly. "But I'd rather be a sea captain. Go on, Tommy. Tell us about your father."

"Well, I don't know much," went on Tommy Todd. "I don't remember him so very well, you know. Then my grandmother and I lived alone. It was in a better house than we have now, and we had more things to eat. I never get enough now when I'm home, though when I was on the fresh air farm I had lots," and, sighing, Tommy seemed sad.

"My father used to write letters to my grandmother—she is his mother," he explained. "When I got so I could understand, my grandmother read them to me. My father wrote about his ship, and how he sailed away up where the whales are. Sometimes he would send us money in the letters, and then grandma would make a little party for me.

"But after a while no more letters came. My grandmother used to ask the postman every day if he didn't have a letter for her from my father, but there wasn't any. Then there was a piece in the paper about a ship that was wrecked. It was my father's ship."

"What's wrecked?" asked Flossie.

"It means the ship is all smashed to pieces; doesn't it?" asked Freddie of Tommy.

"That's it; yes. My father's ship was in a storm and was smashed on the rocks. Everybody on it, and my father too, was drowned in the ocean, the paper said. That's why I like the country better than the ocean."

"I used to like the ocean," said Flossie slowly. "We go down to Ocean Cliff sometimes, where Uncle William and Aunt Emily and Cousin Dorothy live. But I don't like the ocean so much now, if it made your father drown."

"Oh, well, there have to be shipwrecks I s'pose," remarked Tommy. "But, of course, it was awful hard to lose my father." He turned his head away and seemed to be looking out of the window. Then he went on:

"After grandmother read that in the paper about my father's ship sinking she cried, and I cried too. Then she wrote some letters to the company that owned the ship. She thought maybe the papers were wrong, about the ship sinking, but when the answers came back they said the same thing. The men who owned the ship which my father was captain of, said the vessel was lost and no one was saved. No more letters came from my father, and no more money. Then grandmother and I had to move away from the house where we were living, and had to go to a little house down by the dumps. It isn't nice there."

"Does your grandma have any money now?" asked Flossie.

"A little. She sews and I run errands for the groceryman after school, and earn a little. But it isn't much. I was glad when the fresh air folks took me to the farm. I had lots to eat, and my grandmother had more too, for she didn't have to feed me. She is going to the fresh air farm some day, maybe."

"That will be nice," said Flossie. "We're going to Uncle Dan's farm again next year.

maybe, and perhaps your grandma can come there."

"I don't believe so," returned Tommie. "But anyhow I had fun, and I weigh two pounds more than 'fore I went away, and I can run errands faster now for Mr. Fitch."

"Why, he's our grocery man!" cried Freddie. "Do you work for him, Tommy?"

"Sometimes, and sometimes I work for Mr. Schmidt, a butcher. But I don't earn much. When I get through school I'll work all the while, and earn lots of money. Then I'm going to hire a ship and go to look for my father."

"I thought you said he was drowned in the ocean!" exclaimed Flossie.

"Well, maybe he is. But sometimes shipwrecked people get picked up by other vessels and carried a long way off. And sometimes they get on an island and have to stay a long time before they are taken off. Maybe that happened to my father."

"Oh, maybe it did!" cried Freddie. "That would be great! Just like Robinson Crusoe, Flossie! Don't you remember?"

"Yes, mother read us that story. I hope

your father is on Robinson Crusoe's island," she whispered to Tommy.

"I'll tell you what we'll do," said Freddie to the new boy. "When I get home, I'll take all the money in my bank, and help you buy a ship. Then we'll both go off together, looking for the desert island where your father is; will you?"

"Yes," said Tommy, "I will, and thank you."

"I'm coming, too," said Flossie.

"No. Girls can't be on a ship!" said Freddie.

"Yes they can too! Can't they, Tommy?"

"Well, my mother was once on the ship with my father, I've heard my grandma say."

"There, see!" cried Flossie. "Of course I'm coming! I'll do the cooking for you boys."

"Oh, well, if you want to cook of course that's different," said Freddie, slowly, as he thought about it.

"I'm going to ask my father how much I got saved up," he went on to Tommy. "And how much it costs to buy a ship. He'll know, for he sells lumber. You wait here and I'll ask him."

Freddie slipped from the seat into the aisle

of the car. Flossie stayed to talk to Tommy.
Bert and Nan were looking at a magazine
which Mrs. Bobbsey had bought for them, and
she and her husband were still talking to the
fresh air lady. Scattered about the car, the
fresh air children were talking and laughing,
telling each other of the good times they had
had in the country. All of them were sorry to
go back to the city again.

"Papa," began Freddie, as he reached the
seat where Mr. and Mrs. Bobbsey sat, "how
much money have I saved up? And how much
does a ship cost? 'Cause Tommy Todd and I
are going off to look for his father who is lost
on a desert island, and we want to bring him
home. Does it take much money?"

Mr. Bobbsey looked at his little boy, won-
dering what he meant, and he was just going
to answer him, and say it took much more
money than Freddie had saved to buy a ship,
when, all at once, the train came to such a sudden stop that Freddie was nearly thrown off
his feet. His father caught him just in time.

"Oh!" cried Mrs. Bobbsey. "I hope there
has been no accident!"

"If dey is I'se gwine t' git out quick!" cried Dinah. "Come on, chilluns. I'se got de cat!" and she started to run for the door, carrying the basket holding Snoop.

"Be quiet," said Mr. Bobbsey. "Nothing much seems to have happened. We didn't hit anything, anyhow."

Some of the fresh air children were excited, and the two ladies in charge hurried here and there quieting them.

Bert Bobbsey, who was with his sister Nan, looked out a window.

"Oh, see!" he cried. "A lot of men with guns are standing along the track. They stopped the train, I guess. They must be robbers! I'm going to hide my money!"

Several women heard Bert speak of robbers, and they screamed.

"Bert, don't be foolish!" said Mr. Bobbsey. "I dare say it isn't anything. I'll go out and see what it means."

"I'll come with you," said a man in the seat behind Mr. Bobbsey. Several other passengers also left the train. And while they are out seeking the cause of the sudden stop I'll tell my new readers something about the Bobbsey twins, so that they may feel better acquainted with them.

Those of you who have read the other books in this series, beginning with the first, "The Bobbsey Twins," know enough about the children already. But others do not.

There were two sets of Bobbsey twins. Bert and Nan were about ten years old. Both were tall and slim, with dark hair and eyes. Flossie and Freddie, who were about five years of age, were short and fat, and had light hair and blue eyes.

The Bobbseys lived in an Eastern city called Lakeport, near Lake Metoka, on the shore of which Mr. Bobbsey had a large lumber yard. Once this had caught fire, and Freddie had thought he could put the blaze out with his little toy fire engine. Ever since then Mr. Bobbsey had called the little chap "fireman."

Dinah Johnson was the Bobbsey's cook. She had been with them many years. And Sam, her husband, worked around the house, carrying out ashes, cutting the grass, and such things as that.

Besides these, the Bobbsey family consisted of Snap, the big dog who once had been in a circus and could do tricks, and Snoop, the black cat.

These pets were taken along wherever the Bobbsey twins went on their Summer vacations. For the Bobbseys used to spend each Summer either in the mountains or at the seashore. The second book tells about the good time they had in the country while the third one tells of their adventures at the shore.

"The Bobbsey Twins at School," is the name of the fourth book, and in that I had the pleasure of telling you the many good times they had there. Later on they went to "Snow Lodge" and helped solve a mystery, while on the houseboat, *Bluebird,* where they spent one vacation, they found a "stowaway," and, if you want to know what that is, I advise you to read the book.

"The Bobbsey Twins at Meadow Brook," is the name of the book just before this present one. On the farm of Uncle Daniel Bobbsey the twins had had a most glorious time, and they were on their way home in the train when the fresh air children got aboard, and Tommy Todd told the story about his lost father. Then had come the sudden stop, and Bert had seen the men with guns outside the train.

"I tell you they *are* robbers, Nan," Bert whispered to his sister. "Look, one of 'em has a mask on his face."

"That's so," agreed Nan. "Oh, I wonder what it is!"

"Don't be afraid!" exclaimed Bert. "I guess they won't come in this car. Father won't let them."

By this time Flossie and Freddie had also seen the masked men with their guns standing along the track, and Freddie cried:

"Oh, look! It's just like Hallowe'en. They've got false faces on!"

Many in the car laughed at this.

CHAPTER III

SNAP AND SNOOP

THE train on which the Bobbsey twins were coming back from the country had now been stopping for several minutes. There was no sign of a station on either side of the track, as could be told by those who put their heads out of the opened windows. And Mr. Bobbsey had not come back.

"I wonder if anything has happened," remarked Mrs. Bobbsey.

"I'll go and find out, Mother," offered Bert, getting up from his seat.

"No, indeed, I can't let you!" his mother answered. "Your father would not like it. He may be back any moment."

"I don't believe anything much has happened, ma'am," said a man across the aisle from Mrs. Bobbsey. "I can see some men up near the engine, but they are talking and laughing."

"Then they aren't robbers," said Freddie to his older brother Bert, "'cause robbers wouldn't laugh."

"Well, if they're not train robbers why have they guns and false faces on?" asked Bert.

"Maybe they're just making believe—same as when we have pretend-plays," put in Flossie.

"Do you pretend, and make believe?" asked Tommy Todd, of the two younger twins.

"Oh, yes, lots of times," Freddie said. "We have heaps of fun that way; don't you?"

"Sometimes," answered Tommy in a low voice. "Sometimes I pretend I have gone off in a ship, and that I've found my father. I make believe that he and I are sailing together. And oh! how I wish it would come true!"

"Maybe it will—some day," said Flossie softly, as she patted Tommy's hand which was on the back of the seat in front of her.

"I must go out and see what is keeping your father," said Mrs. Bobbsey at last. "Something must have happened. You children stay here with Dinah. Nan and Bert, you look after Flossie and Freddie."

But there was no need for Mrs. Bobbsey

to leave the car for, just then, her husband came in. He was smiling, and that seemed to show that nothing very serious was the matter.

"What is it?" asked Bert.

"Are the men playing a game?" Freddie demanded.

"Is the train off the track?" asked one of the fresh air boys. "I hopes it is—that is, if nobody is hurt, 'cause then we won't have to go home, and maybe we can go back to the country."

"No, the train isn't off the track," answered Mr. Bobbsey. "It's a hold-up by masked robbers."

"There! What'd I tell you?" cried Bert to his brother and sisters. "I *knew* they were masked robbers."

"But only make-believe," went on Mr. Bobbsey, still smiling. "This is a hold-up, or stopping of the train, and a pretend robbery for moving pictures."

"Moving pictures!" cried Mrs. Bobbsey.

"Yes. There is a man up front, near the engine, with a moving picture camera. With

him are some men and women, actors and actresses, dressed up—some like passengers, such
as we are, and others like robbers, with false
faces on. They wanted the train to stop so
they could get a picture of that, for it would
be a funny movie of a train robbery without
a train to be seen."

"And did they actually stop the train?"
asked Mrs. Bobbsey.

"Yes. They held up a red flag and the engineer stopped. But it was all right, for he
knew it was going to be done. It was all ar-
ranged for ahead of time. Now, if you like,
you may come out and see them take moving
pictures."

"Well, who would have thought that!" cried
Bert. "I was sure the men with masks on were
robbers. And they're only taking a moving
picture."

"I'd like to see it in a theatre afterward,"
said Nan. "Don't you remember what fun it
was when we were in the movies this Summer?"

"Were you in them, really?" asked Tommy
as he followed the twins out of the car.

"Yes, we acted a little," said Bert. "There was a make-believe battle being taken near our uncle's farm. We went to watch. They fired cannon and guns, and had horses——"

"And the men and horses were shot!" interrupted Freddie. "Only pretend, of course, but I was there and I was in the movies too. I acted and so did Nan. And I fell in the brook and the man made a moving picture of me doing that!"

"Did they really?" asked one of the fresh air ladies of Mrs. Bobbsey.

"Yes, the children were in the moving pictures a little this Summer," explained Freddie's mother. "It was all unexpected, but we did not mind, for it was all outdoors. It was fun for them." Those of you who have read the book before this one will remember how Freddie and the others really did act before the camera.

"Say, I'd like to do that!" cried Tommy with shining eyes as he heard what the Bobbseys had done. "It must have been great!"

"It was fun," Freddie said.

By this time they were out of the train, walking up toward the engine. About it were men and women, and the children saw a man with a black box on three legs grinding away at a crank.

"He's taking the moving pictures," said Bert.

"Why—why!" exclaimed Flossie as she came closer. "It's the same man who took our pictures at Meadow Brook!"

"So it is," agreed Nan. "It's Mr. Weston."

"Yes, he's the same one," said Mr. Bobbsey. "I told him you children were on the train and he asked me to fetch you up to see him."

When Mr. Weston had finished taking the pictures of the actors and actresses who had to pretend they were being robbed by the masked men, he spoke to the Bobbsey twins.

"Don't you want to act for the movies again?" he asked, laughing.

"Oh, yes!" cried Flossie and Freddie.

"I'm afraid we haven't time now," said Mrs. Bobbsey with a smile. "We shall get home late, as it is. When is the train going to start again?"

"Pretty soon," answered Mr. Weston.

A few more pictures were taken and then the engineer blew the whistle. The moving picture people got in a big automobile to ride away.

"All aboard!" called the conductor, waving his hand to the engineer who was looking from the window of his cab. "All aboard!"

"Come on!" cried Mr. Bobbsey, and he and the twins, as well as the fresh air children, were soon in the car again, speeding on toward Lakeport.

"That's the first time I ever saw moving pictures taken," said Tommy Todd.

"We go to moving picture shows lots of times," said Flossie. "I like 'em, 'specially when they have fairy plays."

"I like 'em too," replied Tommy. "Only I don't get to see 'em very often. There aren't very many nickels lying loose around our house. Sometimes I only make five cents in a whole day."

"Oh, I didn't find out how much money there was in my bank," said Freddie. "I was just doing it when the train stopped. Wait a minute, Tommy, and I'll ask my father."

Back once more the chubby little "fireman" went to where his father sat, and again he asked the question about the money, and about buying a ship to search for the lost sea captain.

"What's all this?" asked Mr. Bobbsey in surprise. "Who is this Tommy Todd?"

"He's one of the fresh air boys," answered Freddie. "There he is in the seat ahead of Flossie."

"He is one of our nicest boys," put in Miss Carter, the fresh air lady. "I was so glad we could send him out to the farm. He lives with his grandmother on the outskirts of the city near the dumps, and, though the home is a very poor one, Mrs. Todd keeps it very neat. She sews for a living."

"Tommy's father was lost at sea, and Tommy and I are going to rescue him from desert island," cried Freddie eagerly. "How much money have I in my bank, Daddy?"

"Was his father really shipwrecked?" asked Mr. Bobbsey of Miss Carter.

"I believe he was, yes. Before then Tommy and his grandmother lived well. We help them all we can, but there are so many poor."

"Tommy can run errands," put in Freddie. "He works for Mr. Fitch, our grocer, after school. He's strong, Tommy is. He gained two pounds in the country. Maybe you could hire him to run errands for you, Daddy, and pay him money."

"He really is a very good boy," said Miss Carter. "If you could give him any work it would be a charity."

"I'll see about it when we get home," said Mr. Bobbsey.

"And you say the grandmother does sewing?" asked Mrs. Bobbsey. "I must look her up, and perhaps I can give her work. We won't forget the Todds."

"But can I help Tommy buy a ship and go to look on the desert island for his father?" Freddie demanded.

"I'll see about it," promised Mr. Bobbsey, with a smile.

The train rumbled on. Some passengers got off, and others came on board. The fresh air children got drinks of water until there was none left in the tank. Some of them crawled under the seats, and one little fat girl got stuck, and a brakeman had to come in and raise the seat so she could get out. Others raced up and down the aisles until the two ladies in charge of them did not know what to do. Mr. and Mrs. Bobbsey helped as much as they could.

"The children don't mean to be troublesome," said Miss Carter, "but they don't very often have a chance to have real fun like this, and they make the most of it. Thank goodness we'll soon be home."

A little later the brakeman called:

"Lakeport! Lakeport!"

"Oh, here we are!" cried the Bobbsey twins.

"Come!" shouted Flossie.

"Hurry!" urged Freddie.

"Don't forget Snoop, Dinah," said Nan.

"I'll hurry up to the baggage car an get Snap," said Bert, for the dog had to ride the.

"Can I help you carry any bundles?" asked Tommy Todd of Mrs. Bobbsey. "I get out here, too."

"Oh, yes, so you do. Well, you might carry that basket if it isn't too heavy for you. But please be careful of it for it has flowers in it."

"Yes'm, I'll be careful," and Tommy slipped the handle of the basket over his arm.

The Bobbseys got out, as did some of the fresh air children, and other passengers. Fat Dinah carried the basket in which lay Snoop, the black cat. She had awakened now, and was stretching out her claws.

"I guess Snoop will be glad to get out," said Flossie, putting her fat little finger in the basket to rub her pet. Snoop purred her thanks.

The baggageman loosed Snap's chain, and let him jump out of the baggage car to Bert, who led him down the platform. There was another dog in the car, and his master came for him, following Bert. And then something happened.

The other dog, who it appeared had been growling at Snap all the while the two were in the car, now made a rush to get at him. Perhaps he only wanted to make friends, but it looked as though he wanted to bite. Snap did not like this so he barked at the other dog. Then the other dog became frightened and ran away, pulling loose from his master.

Straight toward Dinah, who was carrying

Snoop in the basket, ran the other dog. His master called him to come back but he would not. Then Snap, seeing his enemy run, naturally ran after him, pulling the chain out of Bert's hand.

"Go 'way! Go 'way!" cried Dinah. But the strange dog ran right into her, upsetting her. Down she fell. The basket slipped from her arm, and the cover flew off, letting out Snoop. The black cat, seeing a strange dog, ran down the platform as fast as she could. So with Snap chasing the other dog, and with the Bobbsey twins yelling, and with men and boys shouting, there was so much excitement that Mr. and Mrs. Bobbsey did not know what to do.

CHAPTER IV

HOME AGAIN

"COME back, Snap!" cried Bert. "Come back!"

"Run after him," begged Nan.

"I'll get Snoop!" shouted Freddie.

"And I'll help you," offered Flossie, hurrying along as fast as her fat little legs would take her. Freddie was already half-way down the platform after the black cat.

"Come back, children! Come back!" begged Mother Bobbsey. "Oh, Richard!" she called to her husband, "get the children!"

"All right," he answered, but he could hardly keep from laughing, it was all so funny. Dinah still sat where she had fallen, after being knocked over by the strange dog, and there was a look of wonder on her face, as if she did not quite understand how it had all happened.

"I beg your pardon. I'm sure I'm very sorry

for what has happened," said the man whose dog had caused all the trouble by rushing at Snap.

"Oh, you couldn't help it," returned Mrs. Bobbsey. "Richard," she again called to her husband, "do look after Flossie and Freddie. I'm afraid they'll be hurt."

"I'll help get them, and the cat too!" offered Tommy Todd. "I like cats and dogs," he added, and, carefully setting down the basket of flowers, he, too, ran down the platform.

By this time Snap, chasing after the strange dog, was half-way across the street in front of the railroad station, but Snoop, the black cat, was not in sight. Flossie and Freddie, having come to the end of the platform, stopped, for they had been told not to cross a street without looking both ways for wagons or automobiles. And it was while they had thus come to a stop that their father came up to them.

"Don't go any farther," said Mr. Bobbsey.

"But we want to get Snoop!" cried Freddie.

"And Snap will be lost, too," said Flossie, ready to cry.

"That's all right. We'll get them both,

Snap won't go. far.   I'll bring him back.
Where's your whistle, Bert?"

Bert had followed his father, while Nan
stayed with her mother to help get Dinah up.
Dinah was so fat that once she sat down flat
on the platform she could hardly get up alone.
It was not often, of course, that she sat down
that way.   This time it was an accident.   So
while Mrs. Bobbsey and Nan were helping up
the fat cook, Bert gave his father a tin whistle
he carried for calling Snap when the big dog
was far away.

Mr. Bobbsey blew a loud blast on the whistle.   Snap, who was now running down the
street after the strange dog, turned and looked
back.   But he did not come toward the station.

"Come here, Snap!" called Mr. Bobbsey.
"Come here at once!"   And he said it in such
a way that Snap knew he must come.   Again
the whistle was blown and Snap, with a last
bark at the dog which had made so much
trouble, turned and came running back.

"I wish you could call *my* dog back as easily
as you called yours," said the man who owned
the animal Snap had been chasing.   "But I

guess I had better go after him myself," he added. "Your dog and mine don't seem to get along well together, and I think it's Rover's fault. But he has never traveled in a train before, and perhaps he was frightened".

"Our dog and cat like to ride in a train," said Flossie, patting the head of Snap, who was wagging his tail.

"Oh, but we've got to find Snoop!" cried Freddie, who had, for the moment, forgotten about the black cat. "Come on Flossie."

The two younger Bobbsey twins were about to set off on a search for their pet when they saw Tommy Todd coming toward them, with the black cat in his arms.

"I've found her for you," he said, smiling. "She's all right, only a little scared I guess, 'cause her heart's beating awful fast."

"Thank you, little man," said Mr. Bobbsey.

"Oh, Snoop! Did the bad dog bite you?" asked Flossie, putting her arms around the cat as Tommy held her.

"No, she isn't bitten," said Freddie, as he looked carefully at Snoop. "Where did you find her, Tommy?"

"She was hiding behind some boxes down by the express office. I saw her go that way when the two dogs ran across the street, so I looked there for her. She didn't want to come out but I coaxed her. I like cats and they always come to me."

"That's 'cause you're kind to them," said Flossie. "Come on now, Snoop, you must go back into your basket until we get home."

"And don't run away again, either, Snap!" said Bert to the dog, shaking a finger at him. Snap seemed to understand and to be a bit sorry for what he had done. He drooped his tail, and when a dog does that he is either ashamed or afraid.

"Oh, don't be cross with him," begged Nan, who had come along now, after having helped her mother get Dinah to her feet. "Don't make him feel bad, Bert, after we've had such a nice time in the country."

"All right, I won't," laughed Bert. "It's all right, old fellow," he said to Snap. "I guess you didn't mean it."

This time Snap wagged his tail, which showed that he felt much happier.

"Let me take Snoop," begged Flossie of Tommy, and the "fresh air boy," as the twins called him, handed over the black cat. They all walked back to where Dinah and Mrs. Bobbsey were waiting. Snoop was put in her basket, where she curled up as if glad to be away from the noise and excitement.

The fresh air children had gone their various ways and Tommy set off down the street toward his poor home, which, as he had said, was down near the "dumps."

"Wait a minute!" called Mr. Bobbsey after him. "Give me your address, Tommy. Mrs. Bobbsey wants to come and see your grandmother."

"Oh!" exclaimed Tommy, and he seemed rather surprised. "Well, I live on Lomb Street."

"What number?" asked Mr. Bobbsey, taking out a note book and pencil.

"There isn't any number on our house," said Tommy. "Maybe there was once, but it's gone now. But it's the last house on the street, the left hand side as you go toward the dumps."

"All right," said Mr. Bobbsey. "I guess we

can find you. But that's a long way to walk
from here. Aren't you going to take a car?"

"No—no, sir," answered Tommy. "I don't
mind walking."

"Maybe he hasn't the car fare," whispered
Mrs. Bobbsey.

"Just what I was thinking myself," answered
her husband. "Here, Tommy," he went on.
"Here's a quarter. Use it to ride home, and
get yourself an ice cream soda. It's warmer
here than out on the fresh air farm," and he
held out the money. "The ice cream will cool
you off."

"Oh, I—I don't want to take it," said
Tommy. "I don't mind the walk."

"Come on, take it!" insisted Mr. Bobbsey.
"You can run some errands for me later on,
and earn it, if you like that better."

"Yes, I'll do that," said Tommy, and this
time he took the money. "I'll run errands for
you whenever you want me to," he added, as
he started toward the street car.

"All right," said Mr. Bobbsey with a laugh.
"And tell your grandmother that we will get
her more sewing to do."

"She'll be glad to hear that," Tommy said. He was quite a little man, though no older than Bert.

"And I won't forget about taking my saved-up money to buy a ship, so you and I can go and get your father from the desert island," said Freddie, as Tommy got on the car.

"And I'm coming too," added Flossie. "You said I could cook."

"You ought to take Dinah along to cook," laughed Nan.

"Maybe we will; sha'n't we, Freddie?" asked his little sister.

"Well, if we can get a ship big enough for her and us we will," Freddie decided. "But I haven't got much money, and Dinah needs lots of room."

With Snap and Snoop now safe, the seys and Dinah got in a carriage and left station to drive to their home. On the way they saw the man whose dog had barked at Snap. The man had the animal by a chain and was leading him along. Snap growled as he looked out and saw him.

"Be quiet, sir!" ordered Bert.

"Yes, be nice and quiet like Snoop," said Flossie.

"There's our house!" cried Freddie, as they turned a corner. "Why, it's been painted!" he added, in surprise.

"Oh, so it has!" exclaimed Nan.

"Yes, I had it painted while you were at Meadow Brook," returned Mr. Bobbsey. "Do you like it?" he asked his wife.

"Yes, it's a lovely color. But I'd like it anyhow for it's *home*. It was nice in the country, but I'm glad to be home again."

"So are we!" cried Flossie. "We'll have lots of fun here; sha'n't we, Freddie?"

"That's what we will!"

"Home again! Home again!" gaily sang Nan as her father opened the front door, and they all went in. "We're all at home again!"

CHAPTER V

"Oh, there's Johnnie Wilson!" cried Freddie Bobbsey. "I'm going to call to him to come into our yard."

"Yes, and there's Alice Boyd," added Flossie. "I'm going to play with her. She's got a new doll. Come on over, Alice!" she called.

"And you come over, too, Johnnie!" shouted Freddie.

A boy and a girl came running acros the street to the Bobbsey house. The two smaller twins and their little friends were soon having a good time in the yard. It was the morning after the family had come home from Meadow Brook.

"Did you have a good time in the country?" asked Alice of Flossie.

"Oh, didn't we just though! It was— scrumptious!"

45

"And false-face robbers stopped the train coming home," added Freddie. "Only it was make-believe."

"I wish I'd been there," said Johnnie, after Freddie had told about it. "We went up to a lake this Summer. Nothing much happened there except I fell in and most drowned."

"I call *that* something," said Freddie. "I fell in a brook, but it wasn't deep."

"The lake's awful deep," went on Johnnie. "It hasn't any bottom."

"It's got to have a bottom, or all the water would drop out, and then it wouldn't be a lake," said Freddie.

"Well, maybe it has," admitted his friend. "Anyhow, the bottom's awful far down. I didn't get to it and I was in the water a good while. It's a awful deep lake."

"It isn't as deep as the ocean," Freddie said, "and I'm going on the ocean in a ship."

"Are you? When?" asked Johnnie.

"When Tommy Todd and I start to look for his father. His father is lost at sea on a desert island, like Robinson Crusoe, and we're going to find him."

"Take me along!" begged Johnnie. "I'm not afraid of the ocean, even if it's deeper'n the lake. Take me with you."

Freddie thought about it carefully.

"Well, you may come if the ship is big enough," he said. "I promised to let Flossie come. She's going to cook. Oh, no, Dinah's going to cook. I forgot about that. We'll have to get a bigger ship, I guess, so's to make room for Dinah. I guess you may come, Johnnie. I haven't counted how much money I've saved up, but I will soon."

"Is Tommy Dodd going to help buy the ship?" asked Johnnie.

"His name isn't *Dodd,* it's *Todd,*" explained Freddie. "But he can't put in much money I guess, 'cause he's poor. He's a fresh air boy, but he's nice. He runs errands for Mr. Fitch, the grocer. We met Tommy on the train."

"Then f you put in the most money to buy the ship more'n half of it will be yours," said Johnnie, "and you can take as many as you like."

"No, half of the ship is going to be Tommy's," insisted the little Bobbsey twin.

" 'Cause it's his father we're going after, you see."

"That's so," admitted Johnnie. "Well, I'm coming anyhow. I'll put in some money to buy things to eat."

"That'll be nice," said Freddie. "I forgot about eating. I'm hungry now. I think Dinah is making cookies. Let's go 'round to the kitchen to see."

Flossie and Alice were up on the side porch, playing with their dolls, when Freddie and Johnnie ran around to the back door. Surely enough, Dinah was making cookies, and she gave the boys some.

"Do you think we'd better save any of these for the time when we go on the ship?" asked Johnnie, as he took a bite out of his second cookie.

"No, I don't guess so," replied Freddie. "We won't go for a week or two anyhow, and the cookies wouldn't keep that long. Anyhow, Dinah will make more. Say, I'll tell you what let's do!"

"What?"

"Go down to the lake and sail our boats."

"All right. But I don't want to fall in."

"We'll go down to my father's lumber yard, and if we fall in, near the edge, we can yell and some of the men will pull us out. Come on!"

Mrs. Bobbsey said Freddie might go, if he would be sure to be careful. He was often allowed to visit his father's lumber yard, for it was known he would be safe there. And Johnnie's mother said he might go also. So the little fellows trudged away, leaving the girls to play dolls on the porch.

Freddie and Johnnie had fun at the edge of the lake. They each had a small sailboat, and, holding the strings, which were fast to the toy vessels, the boys let the wind blow the boats out a way and then hauled them in again.

After a while, however, they grew tired of this, and Freddie said:

"Let's go up to the office to see my father. He likes me to come to see him, and maybe he'll give us five cents for ice cream cones."

"That'll be nice," said Johnnie.

Mr. Bobbsey was very busy, for he had a great deal of work to do after having spent so much time in the country that Summer. But he was glad to see the boys.

"Well, how's my little fireman this morning?" he asked, catching Freddie up in his arms. "Have you put out any fires yet?"

"Not yet. We've been playing boats."

"And how are you, Johnnie?" went on Mr. Bobbsey, as he patted Freddie's playmate on the back.

"Oh, I'm all right. I'm going in the ship with Freddie to help find Tommy Todd's father who's on a desert island."

"Oh, you are; eh? Well, speaking of Tommy, that looks like him out there now."

Mr. Bobbsey pointed to the outside office. There stood the boy Freddie and Flossie had talked to on the train. He was speaking to one of the clerks, who did not seem to want to let him inside the railing.

"That's all right," called Mr. Bobbsey. "He may come in. What is it, Tommy?" he asked kindly, as the clerk stepped aside.

"I've come to do the errands, to earn the quarter you gave me yesterday," said the fresh air boy, as he came in.

"Oh, there's no hurry about that," returned Mr. Bobbsey. "I don't know what errands I want done to-day."

"Well, I'd like to do some," Tommy said. "I'd like to earn that money, and then, maybe, you'd have some more errands for me to run, afterward, so I could earn more money. I need it very much, and Mr. Fitch hasn't any work for me to-day. I want to do all I can before school opens," Tommy went on, " 'cause it gets dark early in the afternoon now, and my grandmother doesn't like to have me out too late."

"That's right. How is your grandmother, Tommy?"

"She—she's sick," was the answer, and Tommy's voice sounded as though he had been crying, or was just going to do so.

"Sick? That's too bad!"

"That's why I want some more errands to do, so I can earn money for her. She was hungry when I got home yesterday, and I spent that money you gave me—all but the five cents for car fare—to buy her things to eat. There wasn't anything in the house."

"Oh, come now! That's too bad!" said Mr.

Bobbsey. "We must look into this. Here,
Freddie, you and Johnnie and Tommie go
down to the corner and get some ice cream.
It's a hot day," and he held out some money
to Tommy. "I'll let you carry it," he said,
"as the other boys might lose it. Get three ten
cent plates of cream."

Tommy seemed to hang back.

"Could I have this one ten cent piece all for
myself?" he asked.

"Why, of course you may. There is a dime
for each of you. Don't you like ice cream?"

"Oh, yes indeed. But I'd rather save this
for my grandmother. I'm not very warm."

"Now look here!" said Mr. Bobbsey with a
laugh. "You spend that money for yourself
and for Freddie and Johnnie. I'll see that your
grandmother is taken care of. I'm going to
telephone to my wife, now, to go down to see
her."

"Oh, all right, thank you!" cried Tommy.
And then, when he had hurried off down to
the ice cream store with Freddie and Johnnie,
Mr. Bobbsey called up his wife at home and
asked her to see Mrs. Todd.

day, after the three boys had eaten their ice cream, Tommy went back to the lumber yard, and Mr. Bobbsey told him that Mrs. Bobbsey had gone to see Mrs. Todd.

"And haven't you any errands I could do for you to-day?" asked Tommy.

"Not to-day, Tommy. But I may have later. Don't worry about working out that twenty-five cents. I won't forget you, and you'll find your grandmother being taken care of when you get home."

"I'll not forget about the ship we're going to buy either," promised Freddie, as he and Johnnie parted company from Tommy.

"All right; and thank you."

Nan and Bert, that day, had gone over to play with Ned Barton and Ellen Moore, children who lived near them, and they had a good time.

"We want to have all the fun we can while we're at home here," said Nan, "for school will soon open."

"Yes, and I'll be sort of glad," said Bert. "We're going to have a football team this year."

"We'll come to see you play; won't we, El-len?" said Nan.

"Yes, but I like baseball better than foot-ball."

As Nan and Bert reached home, after visit-ing with their little friends, they heard screams from the side porch where Flossie and Alice had been playing dolls.

"Oh, make him come back with it! Make him come back!" cried Flossie.

"Something has happened!" exclaimed Bert, running around to the side of the house, fol-lowed by Nan.

CHAPTER VI

SCHOOL DAYS

BERT saw his sister and her playmate, Alice Boyd, standing on the porch, looking very much frightened. Alice had her doll held tightly in her arms, but Flossie's doll could not be seen.

"What's the matter?" Bert asked.

"It's a dog! A strange dog!" cried Flossie. "Oh, dear! He——"

"Did he bite you?" Nan asked quickly. "If he did——"

"No, he didn't bite me," answered the little girl. "But he ran up on the porch and took my best doll away in his mouth. Now he's gone around to the back yard, and I'm afraid he'll bite her. I called to him to come back, but he wouldn't."

"Was it some dog Snap was playing with?" asked Bert.

"No, it was a new dog. I'd never seen him before. Oh, dear! He'll bite my doll!"

"It won't hurt her to be bitten a little," said Bert with a laugh. "You can't hurt dolls."

"You can so!" sobbed Flossie, who was crying real tears now. "And I don't want my best doll bitten."

"Don't laugh at her, Bert," said Nan in a low voice. "Try to get her doll back for her."

"I will," promised Bert. "Which way did the dog go, Flossie? Tell me."

"He went around back of the house."

"Maybe he thought your doll was a bone, and he's going to bury it," Bert said. "Was she a thin doll, Flossie; thin like a bone?"

"No, she wasn't! She was a nice fat doll, with red cheeks! And I want her back. Oh dear!"

"I'll get her for you," Bert said again.

"I'm glad the dog didn't take my doll," broke in Alice. "I'll let you play with mine, Flossie."

"Thank you, but I—I want my own dear doll!" and Flossie sobbed harder than before.

"Never mind, Brother Bert will get her from the dog," said Nan. "Don't cry."

"I—I can't help it," Flossie said, though she did try to stop crying. Bert ran around the corner of the house. Then he laughed so loudly that Nan knew it must be all right and she said:

"Come on, Flossie and Alice. We'll go and see what Bert has found."

They found Bert looking at the strange dog, who was standing in front of Snoop. And Snoop had her back arched up round; her tail was as large as a sausage, and her fur stuck out all sorts of ways, while she made a hissing sound like a steam radiator.

"What's the matter, Bert?" asked Nan.

"Why, I guess the strange dog was running through our yard with Flossie's doll in his mouth when Snoop saw him and ran at him," said Bert. "Snoop doesn't like strange dogs, and she must have made quite a fuss at this one, for he dropped the doll. I'll get her for you, Flossie."

The little twin's doll lay on the grass where the dog had dropped it when the cat chased after him. For all I know he may have thought it was a bone and have wanted to bury it.

Bert picked up the doll from the grass.

"There she is, Flossie," he said. "Not hurt a bit, and as good as ever."

"Thank you," Flossie answered, hugging her doll close in her arms. "Now we can go on playing, Alice."

They went back on the porch, and the strange dog gave a bark. This seemed to make Snoop angry, for she hissed louder than ever and made her tail even larger than before. Then she walked toward the dog. But he did not wait even to rub noses with her, as Snap did. With a howl the dog ran back and jumped over the fence.

"Snoop drove him away," laughed Nan. "She is as good at driving strange dogs away as Snap would be. Wasn't it funny the dog should go up on the porch, and take Flossie's doll?"

"It was better to do that than bite her," said Bert.

When Freddie came back from the lumber yard that day he told of Tommy's visit, and Mrs. Bobbsey told of having helped his grandmother. Mrs. Bobbsey also told what Mrs.

Todd had said of her missing son, who was shipwrecked.

"Bert, please hand me down my bank," said Freddie to his brother after supper.

"What for?" Bert asked.

"I must count my money and see if I have enough to help buy a ship for Tommy Todd. He and I are going off in a ship to look for his father."

"Now look here, Freddie," said Mr. Bobbsey. "I want you to have all the fun you can, and play with Tommy whenever you can, and I want you to be kind and to help people. I also wish, as much as you, that we could find Tommy's father, if he is still alive. But you must not run off to sea without telling us."

Sometimes Freddie, and Flossie too, used to get queer ideas about what they wanted to do, and once or twice they had run away together. Once it was to go to the circus, away on the other side of the city, and again it was to follow a hand-organ man and a monkey. Freddie's father, hearing him talk so much about getting a ship in which to search for Mr. Todd, thought the little boy might be too much in earnest and would really go off where he ought not.

"So don't start off on any voyage without telling us," said Mr. Bobbsey.

"I won't," promised Freddie. "First I must see how much money I have saved up."

His bank was a kind that could be opened and closed, and for some time Freddie and Flossie were busy counting the pennies.

"Well, how much have you?" asked Bert.

"Flossie says there are only fifty-six cents," Freddie answered, "but I counted seventy. Flossie can't count as high as I can, anyhow."

"I can so!" cried the fat little girl.

"Now children, be nice," begged Mother Bobbsey.

"I'll count the money for you," offered Bert.

"Seventy-nine cents," he told Freddie, after he had finished. "And here's a penny of mine I'll give you. That makes eighty cents."

"Is that 'most enough to buy a ship, Daddy?" asked the little fellow.

"Oh no, my dear boy. You'll need lots more money than that. So keep on saving, and don't go off without letting us know."

"All right," Freddie said with a sigh. "Do you think I'll have enough saved in a week?"

"I can tell you better when the week is up," laughed Mr. Bobbsey.

"School begins in a week," said Nan. "You can't go off on a ship when you have to go to school, Freddie."

"That's so. Well, I'll keep on saving, and when school is out again Tommy and I will go off in the ship to find his father."

The Bobbsey twins had as much fun as they could in the week of vacation that remained. They and their playmates met together and went on little walks in the woods, or rowed on the river. Bert and Nan were allowed to go out in a safe boat, near their father's lumber dock, and Flossie and Freddie were allowed to go also, for they sat very still, and never tried to change seats when the boat was out in the water. This is very dangerous to do, and often boats are upset that way.

Then, one morning, as Freddie awoke in his little bed, he heard his mother calling:

"Come on, little fireman. Time to get up!"

"Is there a fire?" asked Freddie, eagerly.

"No, but school begins to-day and you don't want to be late. Come on then, get up. You too, Flossie."

"Aren't Nan and Bert going?" asked Freddie.

"Yes, but they were up long ago. I let you two little twins sleep longer. But now it is time to get up."

After breakfast Flossie and Freddie started for school together. They were in the same class, and had just left the kindergarten. So Flossie and Freddie set off together, ahead of Nan and Bert. The smaller twins had to do this because their legs were shorter than either Nan's or Bert's and they could not walk as fast.

"Ding-dong!" rang the school bell, calling the Bobbsey twins and other children back to their lessons, after the long, Summer vacation.

"Oh, there's Susie Simmon!" cried Flossie, as she saw a girl she knew. "I'm going to walk with her, Freddie."

"All right. I see Jimmie Brooks. I'll go with him."

The four little ones hurried along together.

talking of the fun they had had that Summer.

A little behind came Nan and Bert. With them walked Ellen Moore and Ned Barton, who lived near the Bobbsey house.

There were merry times in the school yard before it was time for the last bell to ring. The boys and girls played tag, and ran about. Some boys had tops and spun them, or played marbles. The girls did not bring their dolls or toys to school, and the reason for this is that girls don't have pockets in their dresses. Or, if they do have a pocket, it is too small to hold more than a handkerchief. I think the girls ought to get together and insist on having pockets made in their dresses. It isn't fair for the boys to have so many.

"Ding-dong!" rang the bell again.

"Come in, children!" called the teacher, and in went the Bobbsey twins and the others.

"Oh look, Freddie! There goes Tommy Todd!" whispered Flossie to her brother, as they marched to their room. The teacher heard Flossie, and said:

"You must not whisper in school."

"I won't any more," promised Flossie. "I

haven't been in school for so long that I for-got," and all the other children laughed.

Tommy Todd was in a class ahead of Flos-sie and Freddie. He looked across at them and smiled, for the teacher did not mind any one's smiling in school. But when one whispered it disturbed those who wanted to study their lessons.

It was almost time for the morning recess, and Flossie and Freddie were saying their les-sons, when from the next room, where Bert and Nan sat, came a sound of laughter. Then sounded a loud bark—"Bow-wow!"

"Oh, it's a dog!" exclaimed Flossie aloud, before she thought.

"That sounds like our Snap!" said Freddie, almost at the same time.

"Children, you must be quiet!" called the teacher.

Just then the door between the two rooms was pushed open, and in walked Snap, wagging his tail. He looked at the teacher, he looked at the other children, and then, with a joyful bark, he ran up to Flossie and Freddie.

CHAPTER VII

THE SCHOOL PLAY

"Snap! Snap!" cried Freddie, as he left his seat and put his arms around the dog's neck. "Good dog, Snap!"

Snap liked to be petted, and he wagged his tail faster than before and barked. Flossie saw a queer look on her teacher's face, and the little girl said:

"Snap, you must be quiet. You musn't bark in school any more than we must whisper. I didn't want to speak out loud," she said to the teacher, "but I had to, or Snap wouldn't hear me."

"Oh, that part's all right, my dear," the teacher said kindly. "But how did your dog get here?"

"I—I don't know," answered Flossie, while Freddie kept on petting Snap.

Just then the door of the other school room,

in which Nan and Bert studied, opened, and
the teacher from there came in. She was a
new one.

"Is that dog here?" she asked. Then she
could see that Snap was there. The children
in Flossie's room were laughing now. Some
of the pupils from the other room were standing in the doorway behind the teacher, looking
in.

"Whose dog is that?" the new teacher asked.

"He's ours, if you please," said Bert.

"Did you bring him to school?"

"No, ma'am. He must have got loose," answered Nan. "He was chained up when we
left for school this morning, and he must have
got lonesome and come to find us."

"Well, he found you all right," said Flossie's teacher with a laugh. "The doors are
open, because it is so warm," she said to the
new teacher, "so Snap had no trouble in getting
in. He never came to school before, though."

"He's like Mary's little lamb, isn't he?"
asked Freddie.

"Well, he must be put out," said the new
teacher, smiling. "Of course it wasn't the fault

of you children that he came in. But you had
better take him home I think, Bert. And see
that he is well chained. I'll excuse you from
class long enough to take your dog home. Now,
children, go back to your seats."

"Say, Bert," whispered Ned Barton, "I'll
help you take Snap home if you want me to."

"No, indeed!" laughed the new teacher.
"One boy is enough to have out of the class at
a time. I think Bert can manage the dog
alone."

"Yes ma'am, I can," said Bert. "Come on,
Snap!"

Snap barked and wagged his tail again. He
was happy as long as he was with one of the
children.

"Our dog can do tricks," said Freddie.
"Make him do a trick, Bert, before you take
him home. Snap used to be in a circus," Freddie told the teacher, "and he can turn somer-
saults. Don't you want to see him do a trick,
teacher?"

"Oh, yes, please let him," begged Flossie.

The other children looked eager, and the
teacher smiled. The new teacher had gone

back to her classroom with her pupils, except Bert, who had stayed to look after Snap.

"Well, as it is almost time for recess, I don't mind if Bert makes Snap do one or two tricks," Flossie's teacher said, smiling. "But only two. School isn't just the place for dogs."

"Ready Snap!" called Bert. "March like a soldier!"

"You may take my blackboard pointer for a gun," the teacher said.

Snap stood up on his hind legs, and in one paw he held the long pointer. Then he marched around the room as nearly like a soldier as a dog can march. The children laughed and clapped their hands.

"Now turn a somersault!" ordered Bert. This Snap did, too. This was one of his best tricks. Over and over he went around the school room, outside the rows of desks. This made the children laugh more than before.

"I think that will be enough, thank you, Bert," the teacher said. "You had better take the dog home now."

Bert did so, and saw to it that Snap was well chained.

"We like to see you," said Bert as he was leaving to go back to his class, "but you must not come to school after us, Snap."

At recess, which was nearly over when Bert got back to school, the children talked and laughed about Snap's visit.

"I wish your dog would come to school every day," said Alice Boyd to Flossie.

"Yes, wouldn't it be fun to have him do tricks," cried Johnnie Wilson.

But Snap did not get loose again, and he soon got used to having the children away most of the day. But how glad he was when they came home, and he could romp and play with them!

One day Flossie's teacher said to the class:

"Now, children, you have been very good this week, and you have known your lessons well, so I think it is time we had a little fun."

"Oh, are you going to let Snap come to school again?" asked Edna Blake.

"No, hardly that," the teacher answered with a smile, "but we shall have a little play. I'll fix some curtains across the platform where my desk stands, and that will be the stage. You children—at least some of you—will be the actors and actresses. It will be a very simple little play, and I think you can do it. If you do it well perhaps we may give our play out on the laige platform in the big room before the whole school."

"We had a play in Uncle Dan's barn once in the country," said Flossie.

"I was in it, too," spoke up Freddie, "and I fell down in a hen's nest and got all eggs."

Even the teacher laughed at this.

"Well, we hope you'll not fall in any hen's nest in our little school play," said the teacher.

She picked out Flossie, Freddie, Alice Boyd, Johnnie Wilson and some others to be in the play, and they began to study their parts.

The play was to be called "Mother Goose and her Friends," and the children would take the parts of the different characters so well known to all. The teacher was to be Mother Goose herself, with a tall peaked hat, and a long stick.

"And will you ride on the back of a goosey-gander?" Freddie asked. "It's that way in the book."

"No, I hardly think I shall ride on the back of a gander," answered the teacher. "But we will have it as nearly like Mother Goose as we can. You will be Little Boy Blue, Freddie, for you have blue eyes."

"And what can I be?" asked Flossie.

"I think I'll call you Little Miss Muffet."

"Only I'm not afraid of spiders," Flossie said. "That is I'm not afraid of them if they don't get on me. One can come and sit down beside me and I won't mind."

"I guess for the spider we'll get a make-believe one, from the five-and-ten-cent store." said Miss Earle, the teacher. "Now I'll give out the other parts."

There were about a dozen children who were to take part in the little play. They were to dress up with clothes which they could bring from home. Freddie had a blue suit, so he looked exactly like Boy Blue.

One Friday afternoon the little play was given in the school room. The teacher had strung a wire across in front of her platform, and had hung a red curtain on this. Flossie, Freddie and the other players were behind the curtain, while the remaining children sat at their desks to watch the play.

"Are you all ready now?" asked Miss Earle of the children behind the curtain. "All ready! I'm going to pull the curtain back in a minute. Remember you are to walk out first, Freddie, and you are to make a bow and then look to the left, then to the right and say: 'Oh, I wonder where she can be?' Then along comes Flossie, as Little Miss Muffet, and she asks you whom you are looking for."

"Yes, and then I say I'm looking for Mary, who had a little lamb, for I lent her my horn, and she went away with it to help Bo-Peep find her sheep; and now I can't blow my horn to get the cows out of the corn," Freddie said.

"That's it!" exclaimed the teacher in a whisper, for they had all talked in low voices behind the curtain, so the other children would not hear them. "You remember very well, Freddie. Now we will begin."

The curtain was pulled back, and Freddie walked out from one side where some boxes had been piled up to look like a house.

"Oh, I wonder where she can be," said

Freddie, looking to the left and to the right. "Where can she be?"

"Whom are you looking for?" asked Flossie, coming out from the other side of the platform.

"For Mary, who had a little lamb," went on Freddie. "I lent her my horn and——"

But just then there was a crash, and down tumbled the pile of boxes that was the make-believe house, and with them tumbled Johnnie Wilson, who was dressed up like Little Jack Horner.

"Oh, I've hurt my thumb! I've hurt my thumb!" he cried. "Now I can't pull the plum out of the pie!"

CHAPTER VIII

SNOOP IN TROUBLE

SOME of the children laughed. Some screamed. Others looked as if they wanted to cry. Of course the play came to an end almost before it had started.

"Oh Johnnie, why did you do that?" cried Miss Earle, hurrying out in her Mother Goose dress, and picking up the little fellow. "How did it happen?"

Johnnie had started to cry, but, finding that he was not hurt much except on his thumb, he stopped his tears, and said:

"I climbed up on the pile of boxes so I could see better, and they fell over with me."

"They weren't put there to be climbed on," the teacher said with a smile. "I'm glad it is no worse. You came on the stage before it was your turn, Johnnie. Now we'll try it over again."

76

By this time the other children had become quieter, having seen that nothing much had happened. The janitor was sent for and he put the boxes up again, this time nailing them together so they would not fall over.

"But you must not climb on top of them again," said Miss Earle.

"No'm, I won't," promised Johnnie.

"Now start over again, Freddie," the teacher told the little blue-eyed chap, and once more he walked out and pretended to look for Mary. Then Flossie walked out, and this time the play went off very well. Mother Goose came on when it was her turn and she helped Boy Blue and Miss Muffet look for Mary and the lost horn. It was finally found in Jack Horner's pie, which was a big one made of a shoe box. And Johnnie, as Jack Horner, pulled out the horn instead of a plum. His sore thumb did not bother him much.

"Well, did you like the play?" the teacher asked the other children, who had only looked on.

"It was fine!" they all said. "We'd like to see it again."

"Well, perhaps you may," returned Miss Earle. "Would you like to act it before the whole school?" she asked of Flossie, Freddie and the other little actors and actresses.

"Yes, teacher!" they said in a chorus.

"Then you shall."

A week later the play was given on the large stage in the big room where there was a real curtain and real scenery. The little Mother Goose play went off very well, too, for the children knew their parts better. And Johnnie Wilson did not fall down off a pile of boxes.

The only thing which happened, that ought not to, was when Flossie sang a little song Miss Earle wrote for her.

When she had finished, Flossie, seeing Nan out in the audience, stepped to the edge of the stage and asked:

"Did I sing that all right, Nan?" for Nan had been helping her little sister learn the piece.

Every one laughed when Flossie asked that, for, of course, she should not have spoken, but only bowed. But it was all right, and really it made fun, which, after all, was what the play was for.

"We'll have to get up a play ourselves, Nan," said Bert to his sister when school was out, and the Mother Goose play had ended. "I like to act."

"So do I," said Nan.

"I'd like a play about soldiers and pirates," went on Bert.

"I know something about pirates," cried Tommy Todd. "My father used to tell me about them."

"Say, you'd do fine for a pirate!" cried Bert. "You know a lot about ships and things; don't you?"

"Well, a little," said Tommy. "I remember some of the things my father told me when he was with us. And my grandmother knows a lot. Her husband was a sailor and she has sailed on a ship."

"Then we'll ask her how to be pirates when we get ready for our play," Bert decided.

"How is your grandma?" Nan inquired.

"Well, she's a little better," said Tommy, "but not very well. She has to work too hard, I guess. I wish I were bigger so I wouldn't have to go to school. Then I could work."

"Do you still run errands for Mr. Fitch?" asked Bert.

"I do when he has any. And I did some for your father. He says I have earned the quarter he gave me, and I'm glad, for I don't want to owe any money. I'm hoping your father will have more errands for me to do after school. I'm going to stop in and ask him on Saturday. I like Saturdays for then I can work all day."

"Don't you like to play?" asked Nan.

"Oh, yes, of course. But I like to earn money for my grandmother too, so she won't have to work so hard."

Bert and Nan felt sorry for Tommy, and Bert made up his mind he would ask his father to give the fresh air boy some work to do so he could earn money.

It was now October, and the weather was beautiful. The Bobbsey twins had much fun at home and going to and from school. The leaves on the trees were beginning to turn all sorts of pretty colors, and this showed that colder weather was coming.

"We'll have lots of fun this Winter," said

Bert one day, as he and his brother and sisters went home from school together, kicking their way through the fallen leaves. "We'll go coasting, make snow men and snow forts and go skating."

"I'm going to have skates this year. Mother said so," cried Freddie.

"You're too little to skate," declared Bert.

"Oh, I'll show him how, and hold him up," offered Nan. "Skating is fun."

"It isn't any fun to fall in the ice water though," Flossie said.

"Well, we won't go skating until the ice is good and thick," said Bert, "then we won't break through and fall in."

When the children reached the house they found Mrs. Bobbsey and Dinah busy taking the furniture out of the parlor, and piling it in the sitting room and dining room.

"What's the matter?" asked Bert in surprise. "Are we going to move?"

"No. But your father has sent up a man to varnish the parlor floor, and we have to get the chairs and things out of his way," said Mrs. Bobbsey.

"An' yo' chilluns done got t' keep outen dat parlah when de varnish-paint is dryin'," said Dinah, shaking her finger at the twins. "Ef yo' done walks on de varnished floors when dey's not dry, yo' all will stick fast an' yo' can't get loose."

"That's right," laughed the children's mother. "You will have to keep out of the parlor while the floors are drying."

The Bobbsey twins watched the painter put the varnish on the floor. The varnish was like a clear, amber paint and made the floor almost as shiny as glass, so it looked like new.

"There!" exclaimed the painter when he had finished. "Now don't walk on the floor until morning. Then the varnish will be dry and hard, and you won't stick fast. Don't any of you go in."

"We won't," promised the twins. Then they had to study their lessons for school the next day, and, for a time, they forgot about the newly varnished floor.

It was after supper that Flossie asked if Nan could not pop a little corn to eat.

"Yes," answered Mother Bobbsey. "A lit-

tle popped corn will not be harmful, I think.
I'll get the popper."

Nan shelled some of the white kernels of
corn into the wire popper, and shook it over
the stove. Pretty soon: Pop! Pop! Poppity-
pop-pop! was heard, and the small kernels burst
into big ones, as white as snow.

Nan was just pouring the popped corn out
into a dish when there sounded through the
house a loud:

"Meaou!"

"What's that?" asked Flossie.

"It sounded like Snoop," said Bert.

"It is Snoop!" declared Freddie.

"Meaou!" was cried again, and in such a
queer way that the children knew their cat was
in some kind of trouble.

"Snoop! Where are you?" called Nan.

"Meaou! Meaou!" came the answer.

"She's down cellar and wants to come up,"
Bert said.

But when the cellar door was opened no cat
popped up, as Snoop always did if she happened
to be shut down there. Then they heard her
crying voice again.

"Oh, I know where she is!" exclaimed Mother Bobbsey.

"Where?" asked the children.

"In the parlor—on the newly varnished floor! That's what makes her voice sound so funny—it's the empty room."

"Well, if Snoop is in the parlor she's stuck fast! That's what's the matter!" cried Bert.

"Oh! oh!" exclaimed Freddie. "Our cat caught fast!"

"Poor Snoop!" wailed Flossie.

"We must help her!" Nan said.

The whole family hurried to the parlor. There, in the light from the hall, they saw the cat. Snoop was indeed in trouble. She stood near the parlor door, all four feet held fast in the sticky varnish, which, when half dry, is stickier than the stickiest kind of fly-paper.

Snoop, in wandering about the house as she pleased, which she always did, had come to the parlor. The door had been left open so the varnish would dry more quickly, and Snoop had gone in, not knowing anything about the sticky floor.

The big black cat had taken a few steps and

then, her paws having become covered with the sticky varnish, she had become stuck fast, just far enough inside the room so she could not be reached from the door.

"Oh, will she have to stay stuck there forever?" asked Freddie.

"Pull her loose, Mother!" begged Flossie.

"If you step on the floor to get her, you'll stick fast too," warned Bert.

"Wait a minute, children," said Mrs. Bobbsey. "I must think what is best to do. I wish your father were home." .

Snoop, seeing her friends near, must have known she would now be taken care of, for she stopped meaouing.

CHAPTER IX

NAN BAKES A CAKE

"COME on, Snoop! Come on out!" called Flossie to the pet, black cat.

Snoop tried to raise first one paw, and then the other to come to her little mistress, but the sticky varnish held her fast.

"You'll have to pull her loose, Mother," said Bert. "It's the only way."

"I guess she's stuck so fast that if you pulled her up you'd pull her paws off and leave them sticking to the floor," observed Nan.

"Oh, don't do that!" begged Freddie. "We don't want a cat without any paws."

"Don't worry, dear," his mother said. "I'll not pull Snoop's paws off. But I wonder how I'm going to get her loose. I don't want to step in there and make tracks with my shoes all over the newly varnished floor.

"Snoop has made some marks as it is," went

on Mrs. Bobbsey, "but perhaps the painter can
go over them with his brush in the morning so
they won't show. We ought to have shut
Snoop up, I suppose. Let me see now, how
can I get her loose?"

"Telephone to papa," suggested Bert. "He'll
know of a way."

"I believe I will do that," Mrs. Bobbsey said.

Mr. Bobbsey had gone down to the office that
evening to look over some books and papers
about his lumber business, and he had not yet
come back. In a few minutes Mrs. Bobbsey
was talking to him over the telephone.

"What's that?" cried Mr. Bobbsey. "Snoop
stuck fast on the varnished floor? I'll be home
at once. It won't hurt her, but of course we
must get her loose. Don't worry, and tell the
twins not to worry. I'll make it all right."

And this is how Mr. Bobbsey did it. When
he got home he found a can of turpentine which
had been left by the painter. Turpentine will
soften varnish or paint and make it thin, just
as water will make paste soft. Mr. Bobbsey
laid a board on the floor from the door-sill,
over close to where poor Snoop was held fast.

Then he poured a little turpentine around each of the four feet of the cat, where her paws were held fast in the varnish.

In a little while the varnish had softened, and Mr. Bobbsey could lift Snoop up and hand her to his wife. Then he took up the board, and washed from Snoop's paws what remained of the varnish. She was all right now, and purred happily as Flossie and Freddie took turns holding her.

"But the floor is spoiled—or that part is where you poured the turpentine," said Mrs. Bobbsey.

"The painter will varnish that part over when he comes in the morning," said Mr. Bobbsey. "Then we must keep Snoop out of the way until it dries."

And this was done. The floor was gone over again with the varnish brush, and the marks of Snoop's paws did not show. Nor did the cat again go into the parlor until the floor was hard and dry.

"Mother," asked Nan one day, about a week after Snoop had been stuck fast in the varnish, "may I have a little party?"

"A party, Nan?"

"Yes, just a few boys and girls from my class in school. The parlor looks so nice now, with the new floor, that I'd like to give a party. May I?"

"Well, yes, I guess so," answered Mrs. Bobbsey. "How many would you invite?"

"About a dozen. We could have sandwiches, ice cream and cake. I could bake a cake myself."

"Well, you might try. I have showed you how to make a simple cake, that is not too rich for little stomachs. You might bake a sponge cake, and put icing on top. Yes, I think you may have a party, Nan."

"Oh, thank you, Mother. Now I'll write the invitations."

"I'll help you," offered Flossie.

"I'm afraid, dear, you can't write quite well enough," said Nan with a smile. "But you may seal the envelopes for me, and put on the postage stamps."

"Oh, I like to do that!" cried Flossie. "The sticky stuff on the stamps tastes so nice on your tongue."

"It is better to wet the enevelope flaps and the sticky side of the stamps with a damp cloth or a sponge than with your tongue," said Mother Bobbsey. "I'll show you the way."

So when Nan had written out the invitations on some cards, she and Flossie put them in envelopes. Then Mrs. Bobbsey gave them each a little sponge, which they dampened in water, and with that they moistened the sticky places, both of the stamps and the envelopes. And so the invitations were made ready to mail.

"Have you invited any boys to the party?" asked Bert.

"Yes, some," answered Nan. "But only a few."

"Then I'll come," he said. "I don't like a party with just nothing but girls."

"And I'll help Nan bake her cake," offered Flossie.

"So will I," added Freddie. "I like to clean out the cake dishes, and eat the sweet dough and the icing."

"Oh, I want to do some of that, too!" cried Flossie.

"I can see what kind of a time you're going

to have making your cake!" laughed Bert, "with those two youngsters hanging around."

"Oh, I'll take care of them," said Nan, smiling.

"Goin' t' bake a cake, is yo'?" asked Dinah, when Nan came out in the kitchen the next Saturday, which was the date of the party. "Don't yo' all t'ink yo'd bettah let me make it fo' yo'?"

"No, thank you, Dinah, I want to make it myself," said Nan. "I want to show the girls and boys that I know how to make a cake almost, if not quite, as well as you and mother make them."

"Well, honey, ef yo' makes a cake as good as yo' ma, den yo' will suttinly be a fine cook," returned Dinah. "Fo' yo' ma is suah a prime cake-maker!"

"Oh, I don't suppose the cake will be as good as mother's," said Nan, "but still I'll never learn if I don't try."

So Nan began her cake. Flossie and Freddie were playing out in the yard, but when they saw Nan in the kitchen, in they came, running.

"I'm going to help!" cried Freddie.

"So'm I," added his sister.

"Well, there's not much you can do," said
Nan, "except to hand me the things I need.
First I'm going to get everything together on
the table, and then I won't have to fuss around,
and get in Dinah's way."

"Oh, yo' won't be in mah way, honey-lamb!"
said the loving old colored woman. "Jest make
yo'se'f right t' home."

Nan got from the pantry the eggs, the flour,
the sugar, and the other things that were
needed to make a sponge cake. Then when
she had the brown bowl ready in which the
cake batter would be mixed she sat down on a
high stool at the table, with Flossie on one side
and Freddie on the other.

"Now, Flossie, you hand me an egg," said
Nan, and Flossie picked one up from the dish.
She was handing it over to her sister, but her
chubby fingers slipped and—crack! went the
egg down on the floor, breaking, of course.

"Oh dear!" cried Flossie. "Now the cake is
spoiled!"

"Oh, no, not because one egg is broken," said
Nan. "But still we must be more careful.
Perhaps I had better handle the eggs myself."

"You had if you want any cake," called Bert, looking in through the window on his way to play ball with Ned Barton and Charley Mason.

"Oh, I guess we'll make out all right," laughed Nan. She broke the eggs into the dish, and then she let Flossie and Freddie take turns in handing her the flour, sugar, and other things she needed; things that could not be broken if little hands dropped them. But nothing more was dropped, though Nan herself did spill a little flour on the floor.

"Is this batter right now, Dinah?" Nan asked, when she had stirred up the cake mixture with a long spoon. The cook looked in the brown bowl.

"Jest a leetle mo' flour," she said, "den it'll be stiff enough an' ready fo' de oven. An' after it's baked yo' kin mix up de sugar-icin' t' go on de top."

Nan stirred in more flour and then poured the batter into a pan to be baked in the oven of the stove. She carried the pan carefully across the kitchen.

"Don't fall and spill it," called Flossie.

"I'll try not to," Nan said.

Just then into the kitchen with a rush came Snap. He saw Nan with a pan in her hands, and he must have thought she had something for him to eat, for with a joyful bark he made straight for her.

"Oh, hold him back! Don't let him come near me or I'll spill my cake before it's baked!" cried Nan. "Hold Snap, Flossie—Freddie!"

"We will!" cried the smaller twins.

Both of them made a rush for Snap, and caught him by the collar. But the dog thought this was some funny game, and, wagging his tail, he pulled the two children across the slippery oilcloth of the kitchen floor.

"Hold him back! Hold him!" begged Nan. She was almost at the oven now. If she could get the cake safely in it she would be all right, for Snap would not go near the stove.

"We—we can't hold him!" panted Freddie. "He's pulling us too—too hard!"

Snap, indeed, was dragging the little Bobbsey twins right across the room toward Nan, who was moving slowly toward the stove. She could not move fast for fear of spilling the cake batter, or dropping the pan.

"Dinah! Dinah!" called Flossie, to the colored cook who had gone into the dining room
for a moment. "Come quick, or Nan won't
have any cake. Snap wants it!"

I don't suppose that the dog really wanted
the cake batter, though he liked sweet things.
But he thought Nan had his dinner in the pan.

However, before he could get near enough to
her to "jiggle" her arm, and make her drop the
pan, Dinah came in.

"Heah, you Snap!" cried the cook with a
laugh. "Yo' done got t' git outen dish yeah
kitchen when cake-bakin' am goin' on!"

She reached for Snap's collar, and, as Dinah
was very strong, she managed to hold the big
dog, who was barking and wagging his tail
faster than ever. He thought they were all
playing with him.

"Hurry, honey!" called Dinah to Nan.
"Snap's pullin' away from me a little."

Nan reached the oven, and put the cake in,
closing the door.

"There!" she cried. "Now it's all right, and
you can let go of Snap!"

"An' he'd bettah git outdoors where he kin

romp around t' suit hisse'f," added Dinah. "Kitchens ain't no place fo' dogs when bakin's goin' on."

So Snap was put outside, with a nice bone to gnaw, and he did not feel unhappy. Flossie and Freddie cleaned out the brown bowl, on the sides and bottom of which were bits of the sweet cake batter. And after Nan had mixed up sugar and water to make icing to go on top of the cake, the two little twins cleaned out that dish also.

Finally Nan's cake was done. It was taken from the oven, being a lovely brown in color, and, after it had cooled, the icing was put on top. Then the cake was put away for the party.

Everyone one, whom Nan had invited, came that night. There were more than a dozen, counting the Bobbsey twins, and they all had a good time. They played a number of games, ending with hide-and-go-seek.

Freddie wanted to "blind" and look for the others, so they let him do it. One after another the others stole away on tiptoe, while Freddie stood with his head in a corner that he might

not see where they hid. Each boy and each
girl picked out a place where he thought Freddie would not see him.

"Ready or not I'm coming," called the little
boy at last.

Then he opened his eyes and started to look
for the hidden children. The piano in the parlor stood out a little way from the wall, and
Freddie thought that would be a good place
for some one to hide. He thrust his head behind it, to see if any one was back of it, there
being just about room enough for him to do
this. No one was there, but when Freddie tried
to pull his head out again it would not come.

"Oh! oh!" he cried, and his voice sounded
queer, coming from behind the piano. "Oh,
I'm stuck! I'm caught fast just like Snoop,
only worse! Papa! Mamma! Come and get
me out of the piano!"

CHAPTER X

IN THE LUMBER YARD

FROM all sorts of hiding places came running the boys and girls who had been playing hide-and-seek. Freddie's voice told every one that he was in trouble.

"Oh, Freddie!" cried Flossie, who had hidden under the couch in the dining room. "What's the matter? Where's your head?" For she saw only her brother's little fat legs and plump body near the piano. "Where's your head, Freddie?" she cried.

"It's in behind here!" the chubby little fellow replied. "I can't get it out from behind the piano! My ears stick out so far they ~~~~ ~h on the edge of the piano."

By this time Nan had come from her hiding place, and she made her way through the crowd of children who were looking in wonder at the sight of Freddie so caught.

"Oh, Freddie, how did it happen?" asked
Nan.

"Don't ask him how it happened," said Bert.
"Let's get him out, and he'll tell us afterward."

"Yes, do get me out!" begged Freddie.

Bert and Nan took hold of their little
brother and tried to pull him out backward.
But he seemed stuck quite fast.

"Can't you push yourself out?" asked Bert.

"I'll try," said Freddie bravely. So he
pushed backward as hard as he could, while
Bert and Nan pulled.

"Let me help, too!" begged Flossie. "I want
to get Freddie out!"

But there was no room for Flossie to get
hold of her brother. Nan and Bert pulled once
more, while Freddie himself pushed, but his
head was still held fast between the back of
the piano and the wall of the room.

"Oh! Oh! Can't you get me loose?" wailed
the little "fireman."

"We'd better call mother!" cried Nan.

But there was no need of this for Mrs. Bobbsey came hurrying into the room just then.

She had heard Freddie's cries while she was up-stairs, and, guessing that something was wrong, she had come to see what it was.

"Oh Freddie!" she exclaimed as soon as she saw what had happened. "You poor little boy!"

"Oh, please get me out, Mamma!" he begged.

"I will, in just a minute. Now stand still, and don't push or squirm any more, or you'll hurt yourself."

Then Mrs. Bobbsey, instead of trying to pull or push Freddie out, just shoved on the piano, moving it a little way out from the wall, for it had little wheels under it, and, as the floor was smooth, it rolled easily.

"There, now you can pull your head out," said Mrs. Bobbsey, and, surely enough, Fred-die could. The trouble had been, just as he had said, his ears. His head went in between the piano and wall all right, but when he went to pull himself loose, after seeing that no one was hiding there, his ears sort of bent forward and caught him.

"I—I'll never do that again!" Freddie said, his face very red, as he straightened up.

"No, I wouldn't if I were you," returned his mother with a smile. "Never put your head or your arm in any place unless you are sure you can get it out again. Sometimes a cat will put her head in a tin can to get whatever there may be in it to eat. And the edges of the tin catch on her ears just as yours were caught, Freddie. So be careful after this."

Freddie promised that he would, and then the hiding game went on. Only Freddie, you may be sure, did not look behind the piano again, and no one hid there.

"Oh, your party was perfectly lovely, Nan!" said the girls and boys when they had finished their games, and had eaten the good things Mrs. Bobbsey set on the table.

"Wasn't the cake good?" asked Freddie, looking as though he wanted a second piece.

"Indeed it was, dear," said Ellen Moore.

"We helped Nan make it," declared Flossie. "Didn't we, Nan?"

"Oh, yes, you helped *some*—by cleaning out the dishes."

"And Snap nearly made Nan spill the cake when she was putting it in the oven," went on

Freddie. "Only we helped hold him; didn't **we,** Nan?"

"Yes, you certainly helped there."

At last the party was over, and Nan's cake, as well as the other good things, was all eaten up. Then the children went home.

About a week after this the postman left some letters at the home of the Bobbsey twins. Mrs. Bobbsey smiled when she read one, and when Bert and Nan, Flossie and Freddie came home from school their mother said to them:

"I have a surprise for you. See if you can guess what it is."

"Freddie and I are going to have a party!" guessed Flossie.

"No, dear. No more parties right away."

"We're going on a visit!" guessed Nan.

"No indeed. We just came back from one."

"Then some one is coming here," guessed Bert.

"That's it," his mother answered. "Uncle William Minturn and Aunt Emily, from Ocean Cliff, are coming to pay us a little visit."

"And is Cousin Dorothy coming, too?" Nan asked.

"Yes, they will all be here in a few days now."

"Oh, I'm so glad!" cried Nan, clapping her hands. "We shall have *such* fun!"

"And can I have fun with you, too?" asked Flossie.

"Yes, dear," Nan promised.

"I wish Dorothy were a boy," put in Bert. "Of course I like her, but I can't have any fun with her. I wish Cousin Harry would come on from Meadow Brook. Then we *could* have a good time."

"You had a good time with Harry this Summer," suggested Mrs. Bobbsey.

"I like Dorothy," said Freddie, "and I'm glad she's coming 'cause I want to ask her something very much."

"What is it?" inquired Bert.

"It's a secret," and Freddie looked very wise and important.

A few days later Mr. and Mrs. Minturn and their daughter Dorothy came from the sea-shore to pay a visit to the Bobbsey family.

Of course Bert was glad to see Dorothy, and was very nice to her, taking his cousin and Nan down to the store to buy some ice cream. But as Bert was a boy, and liked to play boys' games, Dorothy was better suited to Nan and Flossie than she was to Bert.

Freddie, however, seemed to be especially pleased that his cousin from the seashore had come on a visit. He watched his chance to have a talk with her alone, and the first thing he asked was:

"Dorothy, do you know where I can get a ship to go sailing on the ocean?"

"Go sailing on the ocean!" cried Dorothy. "What for, Freddie?"

"To find Tommy Todd's shipwrecked father. He wants to find him awful bad, and I promised to help. I was going to save up to buy a ship, but Daddy says it takes a long time. And I thought maybe as you lived near the ocean you could get a ship for us.

"It needn't be very large, 'cause only Tommy and Flossie and Dinah, our cook, and I will go in it. But we'd like to go soon, for Tommy's grandmother is poor, and if we could find his father he might bring her some money."

"Oh, you funny little boy!" cried Dorothy.

"To think of going off in a ship! I never heard of such a thing!"

"Well, we're going!" said Freddie. "So if you hear of a ship we can get you tell me; will you, Dorothy?"

"Yes, my dear, I will. Is that what you've been trying to ask me ever since we got here?"

"Yes. I didn't want Nan and Bert to hear. You won't tell them; will you?"

"No, Freddie. I'll keep your secret."

But of course Dorothy knew there was no ship which so little a boy as Freddie could get in order to go sailing across the sea. But she did not want him to feel disappointed, and she knew better than to laugh at him. Freddie was very much in earnest.

Dorothy Minturn spent two happy weeks with the Bobbsey twins. She and they had many good times, and more than once Freddie asked the seashore cousin if she had yet found a ship for him and Tommy.

At last Dorothy thought it best to tell Freddie that there were no ships which she could get for him.

"Well, that's too bad," said Freddie, after

thinking about it for several seconds. "If I can't buy a ship, and if you can't get one for me, Dorothy, I know what I can do."

"What?" she asked.

"I can make one. My papa has lots of boards in his lumber yard. I'll go down there and make a ship for Tommy and me."

The next day Freddie asked his mother if he might not go down to his father's yard. As the way was safe, and as he had often gone before, Mrs. Bobbsey said he might go this time. Off trudged Freddie, with some nails in one pocket and pieces of string in another.

"I can use a stone for a hammer," he said, "and nail some boards together to make a ship. That's what I'll do."

Freddie first went to his father's office, which he always did, so Mr. Bobbsey would know his son was at the yard. This time it happened that Mr. Bobbsey was very busy. He looked at Freddie for a moment, and then said:

"Now Freddie, do you see where James is sitting by that pile of shingles?" and he pointed across the yard.

"Yes, I see," Freddie answered. He knew

James very well. He was the day watchman in the lumber yard, and he walked around here and there, seeing that everything was all right.

"Well, you go over to James and tell him I said he was to look after you," went on Mr. Bobbsey. "You may play about, but keep near James, and you'll be all right. When you get tired come back here."

"All right," said Freddie.

He and the other Bobbsey children often came to their father's yard to have good times, and James, or some of the men, was always told to look after the twins, if Mr. Bobbsey happened to be busy.

"Hello, James," called Freddie, as he walked over to the watchman.

"Hello!" answered the man cheerfully. "What are you doing here?"

"I've come to have some fun and play with you."

"All right," answered James. "What shall we play first?"

CHAPTER XI

A QUEER PLAY-HOUSE

Freddie Bobbsey thought for a minute. He and James had played numbers of games on other days when Freddie was allowed to come to his father's lumber yard. This time Freddie wanted to think of something new.

"Do you want me to tell you a story?" asked the watchman, for this was one of the "games." James knew many fine stories, for he had used to live in the woods, and had chopped down big trees, which were afterward sawed into boards, such as were now piled about the lumber yard.

Freddie always liked to have the old watchman tell tales of what had happened in the woods, but this time the little chap said:

"Thank you, no, James. I want to do something else."

"All right, Freddie. Shall we play steamboat, and shall I be the whistle?"

This was another fine game, in which Freddie got upon a pile of lumber and pretended
it was a steamboat, while on the ground, down
below, the watchman made a noise like a whistle, and pretended to put wood on the make-
believe fire to send the steamboat along.

"No, I don't want to play steamboat," Fred
die said. "But this game has a boat in it.
Did you ever build a ship to go sailing in?"

"No, Freddie. I never did. Do you want
to play that game?"

"Yes, but I want to make a *real* boat. You
see Tommy Todd's father is lost at sea, and
we are going to look for him. So I want to
make a ship. There's lumber enough, I guess."

"I guess there is," said James, looking
around at the many piles of boards in Mr.
Bobbsey's yards. "There's enough lumber,
Freddie, but I don't know about making a ship.
How big would it have to be?"

"Well, big enough to hold me and Tommy
and my sister Flossie and Dinah, our cook.
Dinah's very fat you know, James, and we'll
have to make the ship specially big enough for
her. Will you help me?"

"Why yes, I guess so, Freddie. That game will be as good as any to play, and I can do it sitting down, which is a comfort."

"Oh, but it's going to be a *real ship!*" declared Freddie. "I've got the nails to put it together with, and string for the sails. I can use a stone for a hammer," and he began to look about on the ground for one.

James scratched his head as he saw the bent and crooked nails Freddie had piled up on a bundle of shingles near by. Then the watchman glanced at the tangle of string.

"As soon as I find a stone for a hammer we'll start," Freddie said. "You can get out the boards."

James wanted to be kind and amuse Freddie all he could, for he liked the little boy. But to pull boards out of the neat piles in Mr. Bobbsey's lumber yard was not allowed, unless the boards were to be put on a wagon to be carted off and sold.

"I'll tell you what we'd better do, Freddie," said the watchman at last.

"What?" Freddie asked.

"We'd better make a little ship first. That

will be easy and we can make it like a big one.
Then we'll have something to go by—a sort of
pattern, such as your mother uses when she
makes a dress for your little sister."

"Oh yes!" cried Freddie. "That's what we'll
do—make a little pattern ship first. It will be
easier."

"Much easier," said James. "Now I'll find
some small pieces of board for you, and——"

But just then one of the workmen in the
yard called to the watchman to come and help
him pile some lumber on a wagon.

"Wait just a minute, Freddie," said James.
"I'll be back soon and help you."

"All right," answered Freddie. He sat down
on a pile of shingles, and thought of the time
when he and Tommy Todd should set off on
their ship to find the shipwrecked Mr. Todd.

The watchman was gone longer than he ex-
pected. Freddie grew tired of waiting for him,
and finally said to himself:

"I'm going to look for some wood myself.
I guess I can find it." He looked for some
on the ground, but, though there were many
chips, and broken pieces, there was none of the

kind Freddie thought would be good for a toy ship—the pattern after which the real one would be made.

"I guess I'll climb up on one of these piles of lumber," thought Freddie, "and see if there are any small pieces of board on top. It is easy to climb up."

This was true enough, and once or twice before Freddie had made his way to the top of a pile. Each stack of lumber was made in a sort of slanting fashion, so that the back of it was almost like a pair of steps. Lumber is piled this way to let the rain run off better.

Freddie went up the back part of a pile, some distance away from the bundles of shingles where he had been talking to James.

"This is an easy place to climb," Freddie said to himself. "I hope I shall find what I want on top."

Step by step he went up the pile of lumber, until he was at the top. But, to his disappointment, he found there nothing which he could bring James to use in making a small ship. The boards were all too long and wide.

"I might bring one down, and have James

cut it smaller with his knife," said Freddie, speaking aloud. "That's what I'll do."

He lifted up one of the boards. As he did so the little boy noticed that the pile of lumber was swaying a little from side to side as he moved about.

"I guess I'd better get down off here," Freddie said. "This is too jiggily." He had been told to keep off "jiggily" lumber piles, as they were not safe.

Freddie dragged to the edge the board he had picked out for the watchman to make smaller. The little boy was just going to slide it over the edge of the pile to the ground, when, all at once Freddie felt himself falling.

"Oh dear!" he cried. "Something is going to happen!"

And something did happen. The lumber pile with Freddie on top, was falling over. Freddie did not know what to do; whether or not to jump. He looked down, but neither James nor any other man was in sight; and the office, where Freddie's father was working, was far on the other side of the yard.

"Oh dear!" cried Freddie again.

And then, with a crash, the top of the lumber pile slid over, carrying Freddie with it. A cloud of dust arose and the little Bobbsey chap could see nothing for a few seconds. And when he did open his eyes, after feeling himself come down with a hard bump, he found himself in a queer little house.

It really was a sort of house in which Freddie found himself—a little play-house, almost. The lumber had fallen about him in such a way that Freddie had not been hurt or squeezed by it in the least. The boards had piled up over his head, in a peak, like the peaked roof of a real house. Other boards were on the sides and in front, and there Freddie was, in a queer play-house that had made itself when the lumber slid over.

"Well!" thought Freddie, "this is funny! But I wonder how I can get out."

It was not dark in the queer play-house, for light came in between the cracks among the boards and planks. But though the cracks and openings were large enough to let in the light, they were not large enough to let Freddie get out.

The little boy pushed here and there, but the lumber was too heavy for him to move. Then he happened to think that if he did move one board it might loosen others which would fall down on his head.

"I'm in a little house," thought Freddie, "and I guess I'd better call my father to come and get me out. He'll know how to lift off the boards. I'll call daddy or James."

Freddie began to call. But as several lumber wagons were rattling up and down the yard just then, the little boy's voice was not heard. James, having finished helping the man load his wagon, came back to where he had left Freddie.

"Well, shall we start to make a little ship now?" asked the watchman. But no Freddie was in sight near the shingle pile.

"Humph! He got tired of waiting, I guess," thought James, "and went back to his father's office. Well, if he comes back I'll help him. He's a queer little chap, wanting to build a ship. A queer little chap."

And James never thought of going to look for Freddie, for the lumber pile, which had fallen and made itself into a sort of play-house was some distance away from the bundle of shingles. So James sat there in the sun, waiting, and, far off, Freddie was calling for help. For he wanted to get out, very much.

CHAPTER XII

TOMMY IS REWARDED

FREDDIE BOBBSEY was a wise little chap, even if he was only about five years old, and when he found that he was shut up in the queer play-house, and could not get out, he did not cry. He stopped calling for help, when he found no one answered him, and sat down to think what was best to do.

"It would be nice in here, if Flossie could be with me to play," he said to himself. "But she couldn't get in unless some way was opened, or unless one of the cracks was made bigger. There ought to be a door and some windows to this place. Then we could go in and out, and have fun. And we ought to have something to eat, too," Freddie went on.

But there was nothing to eat under the pile of lumber, and Freddie had not thought to put a piece of cake or an apple in his pocket as he sometimes did when he went to visit his father.

That morning he had thought of nothing much but about making a ship to go sailing with Tommy Todd to look for Tommy's father. And all Freddie had put in his pockets were the nails and bits of string. He could not eat them, and, anyhow, they were back by the pile of shingles where he had been talking to James.

"Maybe James will come and find me after a bit," Freddie thought. "I'll just stay here and wait."

He called as loudly as he could once or twice more, but no one answered him. Freddie made himself as easy as he could in the queer little lumber play-house, and, as it was warm with the sun shining down, pretty soon he felt sleepy. How long he slept Freddie did not know, but, all of a sudden he was awakened by hearing a scratching sound near his ear. Some one was scratching away at the lumber.

"Who is there?" Freddie cried, sitting up.

No one answered but Freddie again heard the scratching.

"Oh—oh!" he exclaimed, shrinking back in one corner. "I wonder if that is a big rat? Rats scratch and gnaw."

Once more came the funny sound, and then Freddie heard:

Mew! Mew!

"Oh! Now I know that isn't a rat!" cried the little boy. "Rats can scratch, but rats can't mew. Only cats can do that! Here, pussy!" he called. "Come in and see me!"

Once more there was a scratching and a mewing and up through one of the larger cracks came a big gray cat, that lived in the lumber yard. Freddie knew her quite well, for he had often seen her in his father's office.

"Oh Sawdust!" he called joyfully. Sawdust was the cat's name; a very good name for a lumber yard cat, I think. "I'm so glad it's you, Sawdust!" cried Freddie.

The big cat came up to Freddie, and rubbed against his legs. The little boy rubbed her back and the cat's tail stood up stiff and straight, like the flag pole in front of Mr. Bobbsey's office.

"I thought you were a rat, Sawdust," went

on Freddie. "But I'm glad you weren't. I like you!"

The cat purred again. She seemed to like Freddie, too. Soon she curled up beside him, and Freddie put his arm around her. And, before he knew it he was asleep again, and so was Sawdust. She had found her way into the queer play-house while wandering about the lumber yard as she often did, taking walks, I suppose, to make sure there were no mice or rats about.

It was not long after this that Mr. Bobbsey left the office to go over to one part of his lumber yard to see about some boards a man wanted to buy. On the way Freddie's father passed the place where James, the watchman, was sitting by the shingles.

"Well, did Freddie bother you much?" asked Mr. Bobbsey. "I'll look after him now, as I'm not so busy."

"Why no, he didn't bother me, Mr. Bobbsey," said the watchman. "He wanted to build a toy boat, and he brought some nails and string. I had to go over to help Jason load his wagon, and when I came back, having left

Freddie to hunt for some boards, he wasn't here. Didn't he go back to the office?"

"Why no. he didn't!" exclaimed Mr. Bobbsey, in some alarm. "I haven't seen him. I wonder where he can have gone?"

They looked up and down the rows between the piles of lumber, but no Freddie could be seen.

"Perhaps he went home," said James. "You could find out by calling Mrs. Bobbsey on the telephone."

"So I could, yes. But if I asked if Freddie were home she would want to know why I asked, and why he wasn't here with me—that is, if he wasn't at home. Then she would worry for fear something had happened to him. No, I'll have to find out in some other way."

"I could take a walk down past the house," the watchman said. "I could look in and see if Freddie was there. If he wasn't, we'd know he was somewhere around the yard yet."

"Well, you might do that," Mr. Bobbsey said. He himself was a little worried now. "But don't let Mrs. Bobbsey see you," he went on to James. "If she did she'd want to know what you were doing away from the yard. Just walk past the house. If Freddie is at home he'll be out in the yard playing. If you don't see him let me know. Meanwhile, I'll be searching around here for him, and I'll get some of the men to look with me."

"All right," agreed James, hurrying off. While he was gone Mr. Bobbsey looked around the many lumber piles near the bundles of shingles where Freddie had last been seen. But no little boy was in sight, being, as we know, fast asleep, with the big yard cat, under the pile of boards which had fallen in the shape of a little play-house.

"This is queer," thought Mr. Bobbsey. "Freddie never goes home by himself after he has come to see me without telling me that he is going. I wonder where he is."

Mr. Bobbsey looked and called Freddie's name, but the little fellow, being sound asleep, did not hear.

Then Mr. Bobbsey told several of his men about the little lost boy, and they began searching for him. No one thought of looking under the pile of boards, for there were many such in the yard. And so Freddie remained hidden.

When he was not to be found Mr. Bobbsey grew more and more anxious, and he hoped that James would come back to say that Freddie was safe at home.

But when the watchman came back he said:

"Your other children are playing in the yard of your house, Mr. Bobbsey. Bert, Nan and Flossie are there. But Freddie isn't with them."

"Maybe he is in the house, getting something to eat," said Mr. Bobbsey.

"No, I hardly think so," answered James, "for when I was going past the house, on the other side of the street so they wouldn't see me, a little boy, who plays with Freddie, came running along. He called to Nan, this other little boy did, to know where Freddie was."

"And what did Nan say?"

"She said Freddie was down at the lumber yard."

"Then he can't have gone home, or Nan would know it. He must be around here some-where. I—I hope he didn't go near the lake. And yet he might, with his idea of boats."

"Oh, I don't believe he would do *that*, Mr. Bobbsey," said James. "We'll find him."

Mr. Bobbsey and the men scattered through the lumber yard, looking on all sides of the many piles. But still no one thought of looking under the boards that had slid off the stack upon which Freddie had climbed. For it did not seem as though any one could be beneath them.

"Well, I don't know what to do," said Mr. Bobbsey, after a bit. "I guess I'll blow the big fire whistle, and get all the men from the shops and every place to help us look. This is too bad!"

Besides the lumber yard Mr. Bobbsey owned a mill, or shop, where boards were made into doors, windows and other parts of houses. Many men worked in this shop.

All this while Freddie was peacefully sleeping under the lumber, with Sawdust curled up near him, purring happily.

Finally, Freddie awakened again, and as he sat up and rubbed his eyes he could not, for a moment, remember where he was: Then he looked down and saw Sawdust, and he said:

"Oh, I'm in my little lumber play-house yet. I must get out. Where did you get in, Sawdust? Maybe I can get out the way you came in. Show me where it was."

Sawdust mewed. Perhaps she knew that Freddie was in trouble, though she did not quite understand all that he said. At any rate the big cat walked over toward a large crack, and squeezed her way through it to the outside.

"That's too small for me," said Freddie, for he could not get even one foot through the opening. "I'll have to find a bigger place."

He looked all over but there was none. Then he called out as loudly as he could:

"Papa! Mamma! Help me! I'm under the lumber!"

Freddie paused to listen. He heard some one walking past the pile of lumber. The little boy called as hard as he could:

"Get me out! Get me out!"

Then, suddenly, a voice asked:

"Who are you and where are you?"

"I'm Freddie Bobbsey," was the answer. "I'm down under the lumber and I can't get out. Please help me. Who are you?"

"Of course I'll help you, Freddie," was the answer. "I'm Tommy Todd. I just happened to pass through the lumber yard. I'm going to ask your father if he has any errands for me to do, as it's Saturday and there is no school. But I'll get you out first, Freddie."

"Oh Tommy! I'm so glad you came. Please get me out!"

But to get Freddie out from under the lumber was too hard for little Tommy Todd.

"I'll run and tell your father, Freddie," Tommy said. "Don't be afraid. He'll soon get you out."

"I'm not afraid," Freddie said.

Tommy ran up to Mr. Bobbsey, who was just getting ready to blow the big mill whistle and call out all the men, more than a hundred of them, to help search for the missing boy.

"Oh Mr. Bobbsey!" cried Tommy. "Freddie can't get out and I can't get him out."

"Where is he? Tell me quickly!"

"He's under a pile of lumber. I'll show you!"

Tommy quickly led the way, Mr. Bobbsey, James and some other men following. When

they reached the pile of lumber that had slid
over Freddie's head the men carefully but
quickly lifted away the boards, and the little
boy could come out.

"Oh Freddie!" cried his father. "I was so
worried about you! What happened?"

Then Freddie told of having climbed up on
the lumber pile, and of its having toppled over
with him, but not hurting him in the least.

"It was just like a play-house," he said.
"And I heard a scratching and thought it was
a rat. But it was Sawdust."

"I saw the cat come out from under the lumber," said Tommy. "But I did not know Freddie was there until I heard him calling. I was
coming to you to ask if you had any work for
me this Saturday, as there isn't any school. I
need to work to earn money for my grandmother."

"Work? Of course I can give you work,"
said Mr. Bobbsey, who had Freddie in his
arms. "You deserve a good reward for finding Freddie for us, and you shall have it. I'm
glad I didn't have to call out all the men, for
if I had blown the big whistle Mrs. Bobbsey

would have heard it, and she would **have** thought there was a fire."

So Tommy Todd was rewarded for having found where the lost Freddie was. The fresh air boy was given some easy work to do, for which he was well paid, and besides this, Mr. Bobbsey gave the grandmother five dollars to buy the food and the clothing which she needed very much.

"I'm glad I happened to come past the lumber pile where you were," said Tommy a little later, when he was taking Freddie home, for Mr. Bobbsey sent Tommy along to see that the little chap did not get lost again.

"I'm glad, too," said Freddie. "I'm not going to climb up on lumber piles any more. But we've got to make that boat, Tommy, and sail off to find your father."

"Yes, I wish we could find him, but I'm afraid we can't. Anyhow it will be Winter soon and it isn't any fun going to sea in the Winter, so my grandmother says. Maybe we'd better wait until it's Summer again before we think of the ship."

"Well, maybe we had, Tommy."

CHAPTER XIII

THE FIRST FROST

MRS. BOBBSEY was quite surprised when Tommy brought Freddie home, and she was more surprised when she heard what had happened, and how Freddie had been caught under the lumber.

"Dear me, I am glad they found you, Freddie!" she cried, kissing him.

"And so Tommy found you; did he?" asked Nan, smiling at the boy whom they had met in the train the day the fresh air children came home from the country.

"Yes," Tommy answered. "I was going on an errand for my grandmother, and the shortest way was through the lumber yard. I thought it would be a good chance to ask your father for work. And I am to have it—every Saturday and on some other days after school."

"You'll earn a lot of money," Freddie said, "and then we can build our ship."

"He can't get that idea out of his head," remarked Bert to Nan.

"Oh, he's anxious to help Tommy find his father," Nan answered. "I wish it would happen, but I'm afraid he never will be found."

Having seen that Freddie was safe at home, Tommy hurried back to the lumber yard office. Then he went on a number of errands for Mr. Bobbsey. The twins' father said, that night he had seldom met such a bright and willing boy.

"Tommy will grow up to be a fine man, I'm sure," said Mr. Bobbsey.

One day, a little while after Freddie had been lost under the lumber pile, he and Flossie were standing in the school yard at recess Alice Boyd came up to them.

"Want some candy?" she asked, holding out some in a paper.

"Thanks," said Freddie, taking some.

"Where did you get it?" Flossie inquired, as she took a piece.

"My sister and I made it," answered Alice.

"How do you make candy?" inquired Freddie.

"Oh, you just put some sugar and water on the stove in a tin dish," Alice answered, "and when it boils you pour it out on a buttered pan—you butter the pan just as you butter a slice of bread."

"Why do you butter the pan?" demanded Flossie.

"So the candy won't stick to it. Candy is awful sticky. Our dog got a lump in his mouth, and it stuck to his teeth so he couldn't open his jaws."

"I wouldn't give a dog candy," declared Freddie. "I'd rather eat it myself."

"Oh, well, we didn't 'zactly *give* the candy to our dog," said Alice. "A lump of it fell on the floor, and he grabbed it up before we could stop him. Anyhow, we didn't want the candy after it had rolled on the floor."

Flossie and Freddie ate the sweet stuff Alice handed them, and thought it very good. That afternoon when Flossie reached home from school, she marched out into the kitchen and said:

"Dinah, I'm going to make some candy!"

"Make candy, honey lamb! How yo' all gwine t' make candy?"

"Oh, you just put some sugar and water on the stove to boil, and when it boils you butter a pan like a slice of bread, and pour the candy in it so it won't stick. And if a lump falls on the floor—a lump of candy I mean—that belongs to Snap. Though I hope it doesn't make his jaws stick together so they'll never come open, or he can't bark. But I'm going to make some candy."

"Now look yeah!" said Dinah. "Does yo' ma know yo' is gwine t' do dish yeah candy business?".

"No, Dinah, but I'll tell her when she comes home," for on coming in from school Flossie had been told that her mother was not in.

"Yo'll tell her when she comes home?" cried the old colored cook. "Yo' won't need t' *tell* her, honey lamb. She'll done know dat yo' all has been up t' suffin queer. Make candy! Oh mah gracious! I done guess you'd bettah not!"

"Oh, please, Dinah! It's easy. You can help me."

Dinah gave in, as she usually did, and got out some sugar, some water and a saucepan for the little girl. Dinah knew Flossie was too little to be trusted alone around the stove, so she stood near herself.

"Let me pour in the water," begged Flossie, and she was allowed to do this. Then the sugar and water in the saucepan was soon bubbling on top of the stove. Flossie buttered a pan, getting almost as much butter on her fingers as she did on the tin, but Dinah gave her a wash rag, so that was all right.

Letting the candy boil, Dinah went about her kitchen work, while Flossie sat in a chair near the stove watching. Pretty soon the door bell rang, and Dinah went to answer it. Flossie stayed in the kitchen looking at the steaming pan of candy until she heard a voice calling to her from the yard.

"Flossie! Flossie! Come on out and play!"

It was Stella Janson, a little girl who lived next door.

"I can't come out right away, Stella," answered Flossie. "I'm making candy and I have to watch it. You sit down on the porch and when the candy is done I'll bring some out to you."

Flossie went to the door to tell this to the little girl, and then she saw that Stella had a new doll.

"Oh, isn't she pretty!" cried Flossie. "I must see her!"

Forgetting all about the candy boiling on the stove, Flossie went out on the porch. There she and Stella took turns holding the doll. All this while Dinah was at the front door. A peddler had rung the bell, and it took the colored cook some little time to tell him her mistress did not want to buy a new kind of piano polish.

All at once Dinah gave a cry and quickly closed the door.

"Sumfin's burnin'! Sumfin's burnin'!" she shouted as she hurried back to the kitchen.

At the same time Stella, who was out on the porch with Flossie, began to sniff the air.

"What's that funny smell?" she asked.

Flossie also sniffed.

"Oh, it's my candy burning!" she cried. "My nice candy! I forgot all about it!"

She and Dinah ran into the kitchen at the same time. Over the stove black smoke was curling up from the saucepan of candy.

"Oh, oh!" cried Flossie.

"Keep away, honey lamb—don't touch it!" cried Dinah. "It's hot! I'll lift it off!"

She was just doing that, using an iron holder so she would not burn her hand, when Freddie came rushing in, dragging after him his toy fire engine with which he had been playing out in the yard.

"Fire! Fire!" cried Freddie. "Fire! Fire! I'm a fireman! I put out fires! Look out!"

Freddie's fire engine, though a toy, squirted real water, from a real little rubber hose. The little fireman pointed the hose at Dinah, who was carrying the smoking and burning pan of candy over to the sink.

"Fire! Fire! Pour on water! Pour on water!" shouted Freddie.

"Look out dere, honey lamb! Don't squirt no watah on me!" cried Dinah.

But Freddie had started the pump of his engine, and a stream of water squirted all over Dinah.

"Oh mah good landy!" cried the fat cook. "Stop it, Freddie! Stop it! Dish yeah am awful! It suttinly am turrible!"

Luckily for Dinah, Freddie had been playing so long out in the yard with his engine that there was only a little water left in it. When this had squirted out there was no more until he filled the tank again.

"Oh my!" cried Dinah, as she went on over to the sink, and set down the smoking pan of candy. "Oh my!"

"Is the house on fire?" Freddie demanded.

"No, it isn't," said Flossie. "It's just my nice candy that burned. Oh dear! And I did want it *so* much!"

"Never mind, I'll make some mo', honey lamb!" promised Dinah, wiping her face on her apron. "But don't yo' squirt no mo' watah on me, Freddie pet."

"No, I won't, Dinah," he promised. "But I saw the smoke coming out of the kitchen, and I knew there was a fire."

"It wasn't 'zactly a fire," said Stella. "But I guess the candy burned up. It's as bad as when we dropped all of ours on the floor."

But good-natured Dinah made another pan of the sweet stuff for Flossie. This did not burn, and it was soon turned out into the buttered tin to cool. And when it was cool Flossie, Freddie and Stella ate it.

Mrs. Bobbsey only laughed when Flossie told her what had happened, but she said she thought the little girl had better not try to make any more candy until she was a little older

The weather was getting colder day by day now. The children had red cheeks when they went to school, and they ran and romped along to keep warm.

"It will soon be cold enough to have a frost," said Mr. Bobbsey.

"Yes," said his wife, "I wouldn't be surprised if we had one to-night. I have brought in my geraniums and other plants."

"A frost!" cried Bert. "Good! That means the chestnuts will crack out of their burrs. We'll go chestnutting!"

The next morning Bert hopped out of bed earlier than usual. He looked from the window. The ground was white, and so was the roof of the porch.

"Oh, it's snow!" cried Freddie, who also got up.

"No, it's just frost," Bert said. "The first frost of the Winter. Now we'll get ready to have some fun. I'm glad to-day is Saturday. No school, and we can go after chestnuts!"

"Hurrah!" cried Freddie. "May I come, Bert?"

"Yes, we'll all go!"

CHAPTER XIV

AFTER CHESTNUTS

BERT, Nan, Flossie and Freddie all came down to breakfast together.

"Well, well!" exclaimed Mother Bobbsey, smiling at the children. "What does this mean? Saturday morning, and you are all up as early as though it were a school day. You haven't looked at the wrong date on the calendar; have you?"

"No, Mother," answered Freddie. "But we're going after chestnuts, and we must get to the woods early."

"So the squirrels won't get all the nuts, Bert says," put in Nan.

"But we'll leave some for them; won't we?" asked Flossie. "I wouldn't want the squirrels to go hungry."

"I guess there'll be enough for all of us," said Bert. "But there will be a lot of fellows after the nuts this morning, on account of the frost which has cracked open the prickly burrs, and let the nuts fall out. So if we want to get our share we'll have to start soon. Nan and I will look after Flossie and Freddie, Mother."

Mrs. Bobbsey thought for a moment.

"Yes, I guess it will be all right," she said. "The woods are safe, and there are no snakes this time of year."

"I'm not afraid of snakes," exclaimed Freddie. "They only stick out their tongues at you."

"Some snakes bite," said Bert. "But, as mother says, there are none in the woods now. When it gets cold snakes crawl inside hollow logs and go to sleep. So get ready to go after chestnuts!"

The Bobbsey twins finished their breakfast, and while Bert found some old salt bags which he put in his pocket to hold his chestnuts, Flossie and Freddie went out to the kitchen where Dinah was working.

"Dinah, where is the biggest basket you have?" asked Freddie.

"And I want the next biggest!" exclaimed Flossie.

"Mah goodness, honey lambs! What am all
de meanin' ob big baskets?" asked the colored
cook.

"We're going after chestnuts," explained
Freddie, "and we want something to put them
in. Here's just the basket I want," and he took
a big one, that Dinah used sometimes when she
went to market.

"I'll take this one," said Flossie, as she picked
up one in which Sam, Dinah's husband, used to
bring in kindling wood for the fire.

"Well, if yo' honey lambs brings dem baskets home full ob chestnuts yo' shore will hab
a lot," laughed Dinah.

Flossie and Freddie, with their big baskets,
went out in the side yard where Nan and Bert
were waiting for them.

"Oh, look at what those children have!" Nan
exclaimed. "You two surely don't expect to
fill those baskets with chestnuts; do you?" she
asked, laughing.

"Of course we do," said Freddie, very ser-
iously.

"No, no!" cried Bert. "Those baskets are
too big. There aren't that many chestnuts in

the woods, and, if there were, and you filled the baskets you couldn't carry them home. Get smaller baskets, or do as Nan and I do—take salt bags. They're easier to carry, and you can stuff them in your pocket while you're going to the woods."

Flossie and Freddie still thought the big baskets would be best, but their mother told them to do as Bert said, and finally the four twins started off down the road, each one carrying a cloth salt bag.

About a mile from the Bobbsey home was a patch of woodland, in which were a number of chestnut trees.

"Oh, look! There goes Charley Mason!" called Nan to Bert as they were walking along the road. "I believe he's going chestnutting, too."

"It looks so," returned Bert. "I say, Charley!" he called, "are you going to the woods?"

"Yes," came the answer.

"Come along with us," cried Bert.

"All right," Charley answered. "I promised to call for Nellie Parks and her brother George, though."

"We'll stop and get them on our way past their house," said Nan, "and then we'll all go on together."

"It will be a regular party; won't it?" cried Freddie.

"It surely will," laughed Nan.

"Only we haven't anything to eat," said Flossie.

"We can eat chestnuts," declared Freddie.

"Too many of them, raw, before they are boiled or roasted, aren't good for you," said Nan. "So be careful."

Charley Mason crossed the street to join the Bobbsey twins, and a little later they reached the house where Nellie Parks and her brother lived. These two were on the steps waiting.

"Oh, hello, Nan!" cried Nellie. "I didn't expect to see you. Charley said he'd stop for us, but I'm glad you did, too. The Bobbseys are going with us, Mother," Nellie called back to her mother who was looking out of a window.

"It's a regular chestnutting party," said Flossie.

"Only we haven't anything to eat," added Freddie, and all the others laughed.

"That's so!" exclaimed Nellie's brother George, who was older than any of the others. "It isn't much of a party, even to go after chestnuts, unless you have something to eat. Wait a minute."

He hurried back into the house, and soon came out with a pasteboard box.

"What's in there?" asked his sister.

"Lunch for the chestnutting party," George answered. "Now you won't have to worry, Flossie and Freddie."

"That's nice!" said the two little twins in a chorus.

Together the children walked down the street, past Mr. Bobbsey's lumber yard, and then they were out in a part of the city where there were very few houses. It was almost like the country. A little later they came to the woods. The woods were on both sides of a broad road, and before the children reached the clump of trees they could see other boys and girls scurrying around, poking in among the leaves on the ground to get the nuts which had fallen down when the frost cracked open the burrs.

"I hope they'll leave some for us," said Nellie Parks.

"Oh, I guess there will be plenty," returned her brother.

The Bobbsey twins and their friends hurried into the woods. Flossie and Freddie were the first to begin poking among the leaves with sticks which they picked up.

"Have you found any nuts yet?" asked Freddie, after a minute or two.

"Oh yes, I've got one!" cried Flossie. "I've got two—three—a whole lot," and she showed some brown things in her fat little hand.

"Let's see," called Bert, and when Flossie held them out to him he laughed and said:

"Those aren't chestnuts. They are acorns. You have been looking under an oak tree, Flossie. You must look under a chestnut tree."

"Aren't these all chestnut trees?" asked Freddie.

"Oh, no," replied Bert, whose father had told him something of the different kinds of trees, from which lumber is made. "There are oak, hickory, maple and elm trees in these woods. Here, I'll show you a chestnut tree."

He pointed one out to the little twins, showing them how they could always tell it afterward by the leaves and bark.

"Look there for chestnuts and maybe you'll find some," said Bert. Flossie threw away the acorns, and she and Freddie began poking in among the leaves again, while the others went to different trees.

Freddie soon called:

"I've found some! I've found some!"

He hurried over to Bert with some shiny brown nuts in his hand. Each nut had a little "tail" fastened to it.

"Yes, those are chestnuts," Bert said. "Now see whether you or Flossie will fill a bag first."

"I've got a whole lot of nuts!" Flossie cried. "Oh, such a lot. Come on Freddie and—Ouch! Oh dear!" she suddenly cried.

"What is it?" asked Nan, quickly running over to her little sister. "Did you hurt yourself?"

"Something stuck me in the fingers," Flossie answered, holding up her chubby hand.

"Maybe it's a snake," said Freddie.

"No, it's only chestnut burr stickers," said Nan. "I'll get them out for you, Flossie. After this, open the burrs with a stick. Oh, look here!" she cried, as she glanced down at the ground. "Flossie *has* found a whole lot of nuts in a pile!"

They all came over to look at Flossie's find. Surely enough, there were a number of the brown nuts in a little hollow in the ground.

"How did they get there?" asked Nellie.

"Some squirrel or chipmunk must have gathered them in a heap, ready to carry to its nest," said George. "Well, we'll just take them, as it will save us the trouble of hunting for them. Put them in your bag, Flossie."

"But won't the squirrel be hungry?" asked the little girl.

"Well, don't take quite all of them. But there are lots of chestnuts this Fall, and the squirrels can find and gather them more easily than we can. Take them, Flossie."

"I'll give Freddie some too," she said, and the two small Bobbsey twins divided most of the nuts between them.

By this time Nan, Bert and Nellie had also found some of the nuts under different trees, though none were nicely piled up like those Flossie happened upon. The nuts were down under the dried leaves, which had fallen from the trees earlier in the season. By brushing the leaves to one side with a stick the nuts could be seen.

"This is too slow for me," said George Parks at last. "I want to pick nuts up faster than this."

"How can you do it?" asked Charley Mason.

"By shaking some down from a tree. Let's find a tree that has a lot of nuts on it, and shake it. Then the nuts will fall down, and they won't get under the leaves. We can easily pick them up then."

"Good!" cried Bert Bobbsey. "We'll do it."

They searched through the woods until they found just the tree they wanted. Looking up they could see the burrs clinging to the branches. The frost had opened the burrs and the brown nuts could be seen, just ready to fall.

"If there was a good wind," said George.

"that would blow the nuts down; but. as there isn't, we must shake the tree."

"It's too big to shake," remarked Nan. "Why, you never could shake that tree. I can't even reach around it."

"You can't shake it by standing on the ground and pushing against it," said George. "I'll climb up among the branches and shake them. I've often done it."

"How are you going to climb such a big tree, when you can't get your arms around it?" Bert demanded.

"I'll show you," answered George. "Do you see this little thin tree, growing close to the big chestnut?"

"Yes," Bert answered.

"Well, I'm going to climb up the little tree until I get high enough to step from it into the branches of the big one," went on George. "Then we'll have plenty of nuts."

"And after we pick up all we want, can we eat?" asked Freddie.

There was a laugh at this.

"Hungry already; are you?" asked George. "Well, it does give one an appetite to come out

on a crisp, cold day like this. Yes, after we
gather up the nuts I'm going to shake down
we'll see what mother put in the box."

George started to climb up the small tree.
This was easy for him to do, for he could put
his hands and legs around it. Up and up he
went, just as you boys have often climbed trees.
He was about ten feet from the ground when
Bert suddenly saw the little tree beginning to
bend over.

"Look out, George!" Bert called. "That tree
is going to break with you!"

George looked down. And, just as he did
so, there was a sharp, cracking sound and the
tree broke and bent suddenly over. George fell
toward the ground. Nan, Flossie and Nellie
were screaming.

CHAPTER XV

THE STORM

"Look out there, George!"

"Jump over this way—away from the rocks!"

Bert and Charley called loudly to the boy who had climbed the little tree which broke with him. But George seemed to know what he was doing. As soon as he felt the tree going over he sprang out to one side, and came down, feet first, on a pile of leaves that were almost as soft and springy as a pile of hay in the meadow.

"Hurt yourself?" asked Bert.

"Not a bit—no. I'm all right," George answered.

"Oh dear!" cried Nan. "I thought sure you'd break your leg or arm or something."

"So did I," said Nellie. "Are you sure you're all right, George?"

"Of course I am. I'll show you by climbing another tree." George who had not ever fallen down walked over toward the chestnut tree again.

"Well, pick out a good one to climb this time," Bert said, and George did. He first shook the next little tree that grew near the big chestnut, and made sure that it was not rotten, which was the trouble with the first one he had gone up.

This time everything was all right. George climbed up, and stepped from the small tree out on the branches of the one where the shiny, brown nuts hung all ready to be shaken down. And when George shook the branches of the chestnut tree, down came the nuts in a shower.

"Oh, what a lot!" cried Freddie, dancing about in glee.

"And one—one struck me right on the end of my nose!" laughed Flossie. "A chestnut on my nose! Ho! Ho!"

"Well, it's a good thing it wasn't a cocoa-nut!" cried George. "Pick 'em up now!"

This the children did. It was better than poking around among the leaves for the nuts, as those George jarred down lay on top, and could easily be seen.

The salt bags which the Bobbsey twins had brought with them, and the bags Nellie and Charley carried, were soon filled with nuts. Nellie picked up nuts for her brother, who was in the tree shaking them down, and Bert said:

"We'll all give George a share of ours, as he can't pick up any while he's in the tree."

"He can have half of mine," offered Freddie.

"Oh, no, little man, not as many as that," laughed George.

"I wish he'd come down pretty soon," murmured Flossie, after a bit.

"Why, are you tired of picking up nuts?" asked Nan, with a smile.

"No, not 'zactly," Flossie answered, "but I'm hungry, and——"

"Oh, I see! And you remember that George brought the lunch," said Nellie. "Well, I guess we can all eat now. Come on down, George, and we'll eat the picnic lunch."

"All right," her brother answered, and a little later he slid down the small tree. The bags of nuts were laid aside, George being given a share of the others, and then Nellie and Nan set out the lunch on top of a flat stump, which was like a little table.

Mrs. Parks had put sandwiches, cake and apples in the box, and there was enough for all. The children ate the lunch and had a good time, sitting around the stump-table. Then Flossie said:

"I'm thirsty! I want a drink!"

"Hum. Well, I'm afraid my mother didn't put any drinking water in the box," said George, looking carefully.

"Well, I can drink milk," Flossie said.

"There's no milk, either," answered George, while the others laughed.

"There's a spring of water over there," said Charley Mason, pointing off through the trees. "We could get some water if we had a cup."

"I can make a cup out of paper," Bert said. "We learned how in school the other day."

With some of the waxed paper which was in the lunch box Bert made a pretty good cup. Then when the thin skim of ice on top of the spring was broken, water could be dipped up, and every one had a nice drink. Flossie had two cupfuls, she was so thirsty.

They played tag and some other games under the trees after the lunch, and then, having gathered a few more nuts, they started back through the woods toward Lakeport.

As Flossie came near the little hollow in the ground where she had found the pile of nuts she cried out:

"Oh, look at the little squirrel! He's trying to find the nuts I took. Oh, I'm so sorry I took them."

"That isn't a squirrel, it's a chipmunk,' said Bert. "You can tell it's a chipmunk by the stripes down its back. It does seem to be looking for the nuts though; eh, Charley?"

"Well, maybe he is," said George. "Here, I'll toss him a few. But there are lots more in the woods he can get, so he won't starve."

From his bag George threw a few nuts to the chipmunk. But the little fellow was not as tame as some squirrels to be seen in the city parks, for they will perch on your shoulder and eat nuts from your hand. The chipmunk, however, made a loud, chattering noise, with a sort of whistle in between and scampered up a tree like a flash of sunshine.

"Oh, he's gone!" cried Flossie, who liked to watch the lively little chap.

"Yes; he doesn't like company," said Bert.

Shouting and laughing, the Bobbsey twins reached home with their chestnuts.

"My, you did get a lot!" said their mother, as she looked into the opened bags. "I never thought you would get so many."

"There are many chestnuts this year," Bert said. "Now we will have some fun roasting and boiling them to-night."

They gathered about the fire after supper, and laid the chestnuts they wanted to roast on top of the stove. Nan and Flossie boiled theirs, but Bert and Freddie said they liked theirs best roasted.

All at once one of Freddie's chestnuts burst with a loud pop, and the pieces flew all over the kitchen.

"Oh my!" cried the little fellow. "What made it do that? Was there a fire cracker in it?"

Before any one could answer him another

nut burst, and a piece of it hit Dinah on the
end of her shiny, black nose.

"What am dat all?" she cried. "Who am
frowin' t'ings at me? Was dat yo', Freddie
lamb?"

"No, Dinah. It was a chestnut—one of
mine. But I don't see what makes 'em pop that
way, like corn."

"Did you make any holes in your chestnuts,
or cut a little slit in the shell?" asked Bert of
his brother.

"No. Do you have to do that?"

"You do unless you want your chestnuts to
burst. You see," explained Bert, "there is
water inside a chestnut, especially a new one.
And when you put a nut on top of the hot
stove the water is boiled and turned to steam,
just as it is in the tea kettle. Then if the steam
can't find any way to get out, as it swells it just
bursts the shell of the nut and sends the pieces
flying. That's what happened to yours, Freddie. I stuck a fork in each one of mine, and
the little holes, made by the fork, let out the
steam. Look here."

Freddie went over to the stove to look at

the nuts Bert was roasting.   Surely enough, from the tiny holes in each one steam was puffing, almost as if from a little toy engine.

"When all the steam gets out and the nut dries, it begins to roast," said Bert.   "You must take yours off the stove and fix them that way, Freddie.   I meant to tell you about it, but I forgot."

"Bang!" went another nut, bursting, and Dinah held a pan up in front of her face.

"I don't want t' git shot no mo'!" she said.

Bert helped Freddie fix the chestnuts, putting little holes in them, and then there was no more trouble.   They roasted nicely, and when they were cool the children peeled off the dried shells and ate the nuts.   Nan and Flossie boiled theirs in salt water, for salt seems to give the chestnuts a better flavor.   In fact, salt is good with almost all kinds of nuts.

The twins "traded" their chestnuts, Flossie and Nan giving some of their boiled ones for the roasted ones of Bert and Freddie.

"I think we are going to have a storm," said Mr. Bobbsey as he came in toward bedtime, having gone to the store for Mrs. Bobbsey.

"What sort of storm?" asked Bert.

"A snow storm, I think. It feels that way, and the wind is rising. It's going to blow hard."

"I hope it doesn't blow the house over," said Freddie.

"I think you are safe," answered his father, laughing.

When the Bobbsey twins went to bed that night they could hear the wind moaning and howling around the house. It gave them a "shivery" sort of feeling, and they were glad to cuddle down in their warm beds. Soon they were asleep.

But about the middle of the night Bert and Freddie, who slept in the same room, were awakened by a loud noise.

"What was it?" asked Freddie in a whisper.

"The wind banging a shutter, I guess," Bert answered. "It woke me up. But go to sleep again, Freddie boy."

Just then the banging noise sounded again.

"Yes, it was a shutter," said Bert. "It has blown loose. I can hear daddy getting up to fasten it."

"It certainly is going to be a hard storm,"
Bert and Freddie heard their father say to
their mother. "It's beginning to snow."

"Oh goodie!" whispered Freddie. "Did you
hear that, Bert?"

"I certainly did."

"We'll have some fun to-morrow," Freddie
went on. "I can go coasting."

"Yes, but go to sleep now," Bert advised.

"I can't, the wind makes so much noise,"
Freddie answered.

The wind was certainly howling and moaning loudly around the corner of the house.
Suddenly there was a big crash on the roof of
the kitchen extension near the windows of the
room where Freddie and Bert slept. Then,
after the first crash, came another.

Something smashed through the glass in the
window nearest Freddie's bed and there was a
thumping sound on the floor.

"Oh! oh!" cried Freddie throwing off the
covers and jumping out. "The house is blowing down! The house is blowing down!"

CHAPTER XVI

THE FIRST SNOW

THERE was noise enough from the howling wind to make almost any one believe the house really was tumbling down after the crash which seemed to have broken in the window of the boys' room.

"What's the matter in there, Bert?" called Mr. Bobbsey.

"The house is falling down!" cried Freddie. "I'm afraid, Daddy! I want to come in with you."

"Well, come along, sonny," called Mrs. Bobbsey.

Freddie ran out into the hall, where there was a dim light burning. Bert felt the cold wind blowing in on him through the broken window. He could also feel flakes of snow on his face.

"Something really is the matter in here,

Dad!" he called. "I guess the house is all **right,**
but our window is broken."

"Did you hear that, Flossie?" asked Nan of
her little sister, who was sleeping with her.
But they were both awake now. "The wind
was so strong that it blew in Bert's window."

"Oh, what a terrible storm," whispered Flossie, covering her head with the clothes. "I
don't like it."

By this time Bert had slipped on his bath
robe and had gone out into the hall. His
father was coming along and, having turned
on the electric light in the room where the two
boys slept, he saw what had happened.

Both large panes of glass in one window
were broken. The shattered glass lay on the
carpet and the snow was blowing in, for the
white flakes were coming down fast now. And
there were also a number of bricks on the
floor.

"Oh! oh!" cried Freddie, who had come
back with his father. "Some one threw bricks
through our window. Was that Jack Frost?"

"I guess it was North Wind," answered Mr.
Bobbsey.

"What happened?" asked Mrs. Bobbsey.

"The wind blew the top of the chimney off," replied her husband, "and some of the bricks crashed through Bert's window. Not much damage done, but the wind and snow are coming in."

"We can't sleep in our room!" cried Freddie. "What are we going to do?"

"I'll close the shutters and fasten a blanket over the window," said Mr. Bobbsey. "That will keep out nearly all the snow. What little wind blows in will not hurt—fresh air in the bedroom is a good thing."

Mr. Bobbsey closed the shutters, and tacked a blanket over the place where the glass was broken out of the window. Then, after he had taken away the bricks and swept up the broken glass so Bert and Freddie would not cut their feet on it, the boys went back to bed again.

It was some little time, though, before they could get to sleep, as the wind seemed to howl ever so much louder now that there was no glass in part of the window to keep out the sound.

"Is it snowing yet?" asked Freddie in a

whisper of his brother, after they had been in bed for some time.

"I'll look," offered the older twin.

He slipped out of bed and to the window that had not been broken.

"Yes, it's snowing hard," he said.

"Good!" said Freddie. "We'll have some fine sleighrides."

It was quite cold in the boys' room, with the glass out of the window, for the wind blew through the blanket and shutters. But no more snow came in and the north wind did not knock any more bricks off the chimney. It was only a few loose ones that had come down, anyhow. Most of the chimney was all right.

It was the first snow-storm of the season, and when the Bobbsey twins awakened in the morning the ground was white and the flakes were still falling.

"Oh, what good times we'll have!" cried Nan.

"I'm glad I have my rubber boots!" said Flossie. "I can go wading in the deep drifts."

"Not until the storm stops some," said Mother Bobbsey.

It was Sunday, and the storm kept up all
day so hard that the smaller Bobbsey twins
could not go to Sunday school, though Nan
and Bert managed to get there. And, as it was
Sunday, the glass-man could not come to fix
the broken window. But the shutters were
kept closed, and with a blanket over the holes
it was not so bad. Bert and Freddie liked to
sleep in a cool room, and never had any heat
turned on in their sleeping apartment. Their
window was always open a little way, except
on the very coldest nights.

The next day a man came to put the fallen
bricks back on the chimney, and another man
put new glass in the boys' window, so the damage from the storm was soon mended. The
storm was over now, though it was cold, and
the snow still covered the ground.

Then the Bobbsey twins had great sport.
They got out their sleds and went coasting on
the hill not far from their house, and when
they were tired of this they played in the snow
in their yard.

Flossie and Freddie rolled two big snow
balls, so large that they were almost as big as

the twins themselves, and finally the balls had in them so much snow that neither Freddie nor Flossie could push them around the yard.

"I'll take them and make them into a snow man for you," offered Bert. He put one snow ball on top of the other, Charley Mason helping him lift it, and then they made a third, smaller ball for the man's head.

Pieces of coal made eyes and nose for the snow man, and Nan gave Bert a bit of her red hair ribbon which, when fastened on the snow face, made it look exactly as if the snow man was sticking out his tongue at you.

His arms were made of long rolls of snow, and one was crossed on his chest, holding a broom. An old hat of Mr. Bobbsey's on top of the snow man's head made him look quite natural.

"Now you can finish the rest of him," said Bert to Flossie and Freddie. "Get some more pieces of coal, and put them down the front."

"What for?" Flossie asked.

"They will look like buttons on his overcoat," answered Bert.

"Oh, let's do it!" cried Freddie.

They did, and when they had finished putting a row of pieces of coal down the front of the snow man, they looked just as Bert had said they would—like buttons on a coat.

"Now let's make a little snow image, and he will be the snow man's little boy," said Freddie, after a bit.

"Oh, that will be nice!" cried Flossie.

The little twins rolled some smaller balls of snow, and, putting them together, as they had seen Bert do, they soon had a little snow boy, which stood beside the big snow man.

While the smaller Bobbsey twins were doing this Bert and Charley were making a snow fort in the back yard. And when it was finished some other boys came along and there was a snow battle. Bert and Charley, inside the fort, threw snowballs at the other boys outside. And every time they threw, Bert and Charley would dodge down behind the walls of the fort, so they were not hit very often.

But finally so many boys crowded around the snow fort, throwing balls from all sides at Bert and Charley, that they could not throw back fast enough, and they had to give up.

"Whoop! Come on, capture the fort!" cried Ned Barton.

Over the walls swarmed the boys, and Bert and Charley were taken "prisoners." Of course it was only in fun, and only soft snowballs, which hurt no one, were used, and all had a good time.

Then other boys took a turn inside the fort, while their chums threw snowballs at them from outside the walls, and the game went on this way, by turns.

"I'm glad it snowed," said Jimmie Heath.

"So am I," added Bert. "We can have such fun. I say, why not build a snow house?" he asked, after they had become tired of playing fort. "The snow is just right for packing."

"All right—a snow house!" cried the other boys. "We'll make one!"

They made a big pile of snow, using some of that which was in the walls of the fort. When the pile was large enough they began to dig out a place inside. This was to be the hollow part of the house, or the main room where they would stay.

Some boys worked at the outside walls, making them straight and smooth, while others took away the snow that Bert and Charlie dug from the inside.

The roof of the snow house was rounding, just like those of the snow houses made by the Eskimos in the arctic region. And finally, when Bert and Charley had the inside scooped out enough for more boys to get in, they all entered and sat about on some boxes which Bert found in the cellar.

The snow house was enjoyed by the boys and the Bobbsey twins for some days. But the sun was melting the snow a little every day, and one afternoon, when Flossie and Freddie came home from school early, and went out to play in the snow house, something happened.

Before long Flossie went to the kitchen to ask Dinah for some cookies to have a make-believe party in the snow house, and when the cook had given them to her, and the little girl was about to come out, she looked from the window and saw a strange sight.

Snap was playing about the yard with another dog. All of a sudden Snap gave a jump, right on top of the snow house, and he was so heavy, and the roof was so thin, that it caved in. Snap, with a bark, jumped away and ran off with the other dog, but Freddie was held fast by the pile of snow which fell on him, as he was inside.

"Oh! oh!" cried the little fellow, his voice muffled by the pile of snow. "Help me out! Help me out! I'm buried under the snow house! Help me out! Oh, Flossie!"

CHAPTER XVII

ON THE HILL

"Dinah! Dinah!" called Flossie, dropping to the floor the cookies she had gotten to take out to the snow house. "Oh, Dinah! Look at Freddie!"

Dinah hurried to the window.

"Freddie?" she asked. "Freddie? Where am Freddie? I can't see him, so how kin I look at him, Flossie lamb?"

"Oh, you can't see him!" wailed Flossie. "But you can hear him, can't you?"

Dinah listened.

"Help me out! Help me out!" Freddie was crying. His voice was rather faint, for he was under the snow, and it sounded as though he were down in the cellar. But though the snow roof had fallen in when Snap jumped on it, there was a sort of little cave, or hollow around his head so Freddie could call out.

"Don't you hear him?" asked Flossie, who was so excited she did not know what to do. "Don't you hear him, Dinah?"

"Yes, I *heahs* him all right," replied the colored cook, "but I can't *see* him, honey lamb."

"He's under the snow! In the snow house!" Flossie went on. "The roof fell on him because Snap jumped on it when I came in here to get the cookies. Oh, Dinah, will you help get him out?"

"Git Freddie lamb out? Course I will! In de snow house wid de roof fell in on him! Oh mah land ob massy!" cried Dinah. "It's jest laik it done happened once befo' when Bert made a bigger house."

She caught up a big spoon, which she used to stir the pancakes, and rushed out to the yard, Flossie running after her. Up to the big pile of snow, which did not look much like a house now, ran the cook. Then, just as she might have stirred a cake with the big spoon, she began digging in the snow. It was almost as good as a shovel.

In a little while Freddie's head was uncovered, and then it was easy to get him out. He wasn't hurt a bit, only a little scared, and he laughed when Dinah and Flossie brushed the snow off him.

"But you can't brush out what's down my neck, inside my coat," he said, squirming about. "It's cold, and it tickles."

"Snow down inside your clo'hes!" exclaimed Dinah. "Den yo' got t' come right in de house an' hab it tucken out. You'll ketch cold ef yo' don't."

"Maybe you could get it out if you stood me on my head and wiggled me," Freddie said, after thinking about it. "Could you try that, Dinah?"

"Try what, honey lamb?"

"Take hold of my feet, you and Flossie, and stand me on my head. Then the snow will run down from under my coat and I won't have to go in and undress. I don't want to do that. I want to build the snow house up again."

Dinah laughed.

"Ho! ho!" she said. "I'm not gwine t' do such t'ing as dat! No, sah! Yo' come in de house an' git dry t'ings on," and with that she caught Freddie up under one arm and marched him into the house, where he soon changed into dry clothes.

"Now you can go out to play again," his mother said, "but don't go in any snow houses unless you are sure the roof is thick enough to keep from falling in on you. The sun is so warm now, I don't believe it will be safe to make snow houses. Play at something else."

"All right, Mother, we will," promised Flossie and Freddie.

They took the cookies which Flossie had forgotten about in the excitement and, after eating them, the two children made another snow man; for the first one, and his "little boy" as they called him, had melted into mere lumps.

For about a week the weather was warm, and most of the first snow melted. Then came another storm, which covered the ground deep with white flakes, and once more the coasting hill was lively with the shouting, laughing and merry boys and girls.

Flossie and Freddie, as well as Nan and Bert, spent as much time on the coasting hill as their mother would let them. After school every day they were out with their sleds, and on Saturday they were only home for their meals.

Bert and Charley Mason had made a bob-sled, by fastening two sleds together with a long plank. This they covered with a piece of carpet. On this eight or nine boys or girls could sit, while Bert or Charley steered the bob down the hill by a wheel fastened to the front sled.

On the back sled was a bell to warn other coasters out of the way, and sometimes, when there were not many on the hill, Freddie was allowed to sit on the rear sled and ring the bell. He liked that.

Flossie and Freddie each had sleds of their own, and they rode down on them alone, on one side of the hill where the smaller boys and girls kept by themselves.

"For," said Alice Boyd, "we don't want to get run over by the big bob."

"I guess not!" cried Johnnie Wilson. "Some day we'll make a bob ourselves, Freddie."

"That's what we will."

The Bobbsey twins were coasting one day after school, when Freddie saw, walking up the hill, Tommy Todd, the fresh air boy. Tommy looked tired, for he had just been doing some errands for Mr. Bobbsey.

"Hello, Tommy!" called Freddie. "Why don't you get your sled and have a coast? It's lots of fun."

"Yes, I guess it is," said Tommy, with a smile.

"Then go and get your sled," said Freddie again.

"No, I don't believe I will," Tommy said. And he said it in such a queer way that Nan Bobbsey whispered to Bert:

"I don't believe he has a sled, and he doesn't want to say so."

"I guess that's right," Bert replied. "I'll offer him a ride on our bob."

"That will be nice," Nan said. "He can have my place," for she had been coasting with her brother.

"Wouldn't you like to ride down with us?" asked Bert, of Tommy.

"Wouldn't I though?" cried Tommy, his eyes shining. "Well, I guess I would!"

"Come on, then," cried Bert.

"He can ride on my sled, too," said Freddie.
"And on mine!" added Flossie.

"I guess your sleds are too small," Bert said,
with a smile, for Tommy was even bigger than
Bert, and Bert could not fit on the sleds of
his younger brother and sister any more.

"Thank you, just the same," said Tommy to
the little Bobbsey twins. "I'll go down on the
big bob. But I'll pull your sleds up the hill for
you."

"That will be nice," declared Flossie. "I
like riding down hill, but I don't like walking
up, and pulling my sled."

Room was made for Tommy on the big bob-
sled and he was soon gliding down the long
hill, Bert steering. Once or twice the smaller
boys or girls, on their little sleds, would edge
over toward that part of the hill where the big
boys and girls, with their sleds or bob-sleds,
were coasting.

"Keep out of the way, little folks!" warned
Bert. "There's room enough for you on your
own side, and you might be hurt."

"And you two be careful," said Nan to
Flossie and Freddie. "Stay on your own side."

The two small twins said they would do so.

"Now for a last coast!" cried Bert, when Tommy had been given a number of rides on the bob-sled. "It's time to go home to supper."

"Maybe we can come out after supper," said Nan. "There's going to be a lovely moon, and coasting by moonlight is fine."

"Maybe we can," Bert said. "Come on, Tommy," he called. "This is our last coast before supper."

"All right," Tommy answered. He had walked up the hill, pulling after him the sleds of Flossie and Freddie, who liked to have him help them in this way.

"Last coast, little ones!" Bert called to the small twins. "Then it's time to go home."

"Whose turn is it to steer?" asked Charley Mason.

"Yours, I guess," Bert answered. "Tommy, you can sit right behind Charley and watch how he does it. Then next time you come out on this hill we'll let you steer."

"Thanks!" exclaimed Tommy. He had been anxious to take hold of the wheel himself, but he did not like to ask.

On the bob-sled the boys and girls took their seats. Bert was on the back sled, to push off and ring tne bell.

"All ready?" he called.

"All ready," answered Charley.

Bert gave a push and the bob-sled started down hill. On either side were other bob-sleds and single sleds, while farther off, to the right, were streams of smaller boys and girls.

Clang! Clang! went the bell, as Bert rang it.

The bob-sled was about half-way down the hill when Nan, sitting next to Tommy, who was behind Charley, gave a cry.

"Oh, look!" Nan exclaimed. "Flossie and Freddie! They're going to get right in our way! Steer out, Charley!"

The little Bobbseys, in taking their last coast, had come too near the part of the hill where the big sleds were.

"Flossie! Freddie!" cried Nan. "Look out! Steer away!"

But they did not seem able to do it.

"I guess we won't run into them," Charley said. He was trying as hard as he could to keep to one side.

All at once the bob-sled struck a lump of ice, and the front sled jumped into the air. Charley Mason was jarred so hard that he rolled off. The bob-sled swayed from side to side when no one was steering it.

Then Flossie and Freddie, on their sleds, steered right over in the way of the bob-sled. They could not help it, they said afterward, and that was probably true, for they did not know much about steering sleds.

"Oh!" cried Nan. "We'll run right over them."

But Tommy Todd, who was sitting behind Charley, slid forward as the other boy rolled off, and now Tommy grasped the steering wheel with all his might.

He twisted it around, to send the bob-sled away from Flossie and Freddie, who were almost under the runners now. Bert, who saw what was about to happen, was ringing the bell as hard as he could. The other boys were yelling and the girls were screaming.

"Flossie! Freddie! Fall off your sleds Roll out of the way!" yelled Nan.

CHAPTER XVIII

BERT'S SNOWSHOES

FOR a moment it seemed as though there would be an accident, in which not only Flossie and Freddie, but some of those on the big bob-sled as well, would be hurt. But Tommy Todd seemed to know just what to do.

"It's all right!" he cried. "Stay on your sleds, Freddie and Flossie. I can steer out of your way."

And Tommy did. But the only way he could avoid hitting the two little twins was to steer the big bob-sled into a bank of soft snow on one side of the hill. This he did, and though he, Nan and some of those sitting in front were covered with a shower of the white flakes, no one was hurt. Flossie and Freddie kept on down the hill on their sleds, scared, but not in the least harmed.

"Say, it's a good thing you grabbed that

steering wheel when you did," said Bert to Tommy, as they all got off the bob-sled.

"I should say so!" cried Ned Barton. "I didn't know you could steer, Tommy."

"I didn't know it myself until I tried," Tommy said, with a smile, as he dug some snow out of his ear. "I knew I just *had* to steer, though, when I saw Charley fall off. We didn't want to run over Flossie and Freddie."

"It's a good thing you sat so close to the steering wheel," put in Nan. "You grabbed it just in time."

Flossie and Freddie came walking up the hill, and Charley, who had picked himself up, came walking down. He had not been hurt by his fall.

"Flossie—Freddie, what made you steer over to our side?" asked Bert.

"We couldn't help it," said Freddie.

"Our sleds just did it themselves," went on Flossie. "Did you think we were going to run into you?"

"No, but we almost ran into *you!*" exclaimed Nan. "You must be more careful or mother won't let you come out on the hill again."

"Well, we're tired of coasting now, anyhow," Freddie said. "We're going home."

Most of the others made ready to go home also, for it was nearly supper time.

"That was a fine thing you did—saving my little brother and sister from getting hurt, Tommy," said Bert, as he walked along, pulling the bob-sled after him. "I'll tell my father and mother what you did."

"Oh, that wasn't anything," Tommy said. "Anybody would have done the same if he had been in my place."

"Yes, but not everybody would have steered as quickly as you did. You surely can steer a bob! The next time you come out on the hill I'll let you steer a lot."

"Thanks," answered Tommy.

Mr. Bobbsey was very much pleased that night when he learned how good Tommy had been.

"I must keep an eye on that boy," he said. "I think he will make a good man. I'll help him all I can. He is so anxious to run errands and do work about the lumber yard to earn money. How is his grandmother?" Mr. Bobbsey asked his wife. "Have you been to see her lately?"

"Yes, but she isn't very well. She can't sew as much as she used to, but some ladies and myself are looking after her. Oh, I don't like to think of the danger Flossie and Freddie were in on that hill!"

"Oh, well, maybe they wouldn't have been hurt much," said Bert.

"Just the same, I think they would be safer on a little hill of their own," said Mr. Bobbsey. "Can't you find one for them, Bert?"

"Yes, I guess I could make a hill in the back yard for them."

"Make a hill? Why, Bert Bobbsey, nobody can *make* a hill!" cried Freddie. "It just has to *grow.*"

"Well, I think I can make one. Just wait," was what Bert said.

The next Saturday he was busy in the back yard with some boards, a hammer and some nails.

"What are you doing?" asked Freddie, who had gotten up later than usual that morning.

"Making a little hill for you and Flossie."

"You can't do it," said Freddie. "Nobody can *make* a hill!"

But he watched what his brother was doing. Bert set some posts in the ground, though it was hard to dig, for the earth was frozen. But the posts did not have to go in ~~very deep~~. From the top of the posts to the ground Bert next slanted two long boards, bracing them on the under side with shorter posts. Then he made a little platform by nailing boards from the tops of the first two posts to two others which he placed a little back of them.

"Why say, that does begin to look like a hill!" exclaimed Freddie, for the slanting boards were just like a slanting hill of earth. "Only you can't slide down on that 'cause it hasn't any snow on," he said.

"Well, it's easy enough to shovel some snow on, and pack it down hard," answered Bert. "You get your shovel and begin."

Freddie was delighted to do this, and was soon tossing up on the slanting boards shovelful after shovelful of snow. When Bert had finished nailing the platform on top of the posts, which were about seven feet high, he helped Freddie pile on the snow. When Flossie came out, after her brothers had been working for some time, the little girl cried:

"Oh, how did that hill get in our yard?" for by this time all the wood had been covered with the snow Freddie and Bert had piled on.

"Bert *made* the hill," said Freddie, proudly. "I didn't think he could do it, but he did. I thought hills had to grow."

"It's nice," said Flossie. "But how are we going to walk up to the top to slide down?"

The hill Bert had built was steep. He had made it that way as it had to be short, and he wanted the little coasters to get a "good start."

"I'll fix it so you can get to the top," Bert said. He got some boxes and piled them up, like steps. On these Flossie and Freddie could get on the little square platform which was at the top of the wooden hill, now covered with snow. They could pull their sleds up after them.

At the foot of the hill Bert, with Flossie and Freddie to help him, smoothed out the snow all the way across the yard, packing it hard so the sleds would glide over it easily.

"To-night we'll put some water on and let it freeze," Bert said. "Then you'll have a dandy hill, all your own, and you'll be in no danger from our big bob."

"That's fine!" cried Freddie.

"May we slide down it now?" asked Flossie.

"Yes," Bert told her. She had the first coast. There was only room for one at a time on the hill Bert made, so they had to take turns. Flossie sat on her sled on top of the little platform, and pushed herself off. Down she went with a whizz, half way across the yard.

"Oh, it's fine!" she cried. "I want to coast again!"

"It's Freddie's turn now," said Bert, and down went Freddie.

Then the Bobbsey twins had lots of fun on the "made" hill. They invited Johnnie Wilson and Alice Boyd over to coast with them, and the four little ones had a grand time.

"And they are in no danger, that is the nicest part of it," Mrs. Bobbsey said. "I don't have to worry about them now. I'm so glad you built the hill, Bert."

"I'm going to build something else, too," said Bert.

"What?" asked Nan.

"Snowshoes," was his answer.

"What are snowshoes?" Freddie demanded.

"Shoes made so you can walk on top of the soft snow instead of sinking down in it," Bert replied. "Of course I can't make the kind the Indians and hunters make, which look something like lawn tennis rackets, but I know how to make another kind. I saw a picture of them in a book."

But before Bert started to make his snowshoes he made the little hill better for coasting. That night he poured water on the snow that covered it, and, as the weather was cold, the water and snow froze into a glaring stretch of ice.

And my! how Flossie and Freddie did whizz down the hill on their sleds then. It was perfectly safe, though, for Bert had put little strips of wood on the edges of the wooden hill, so the sleds would not slide off to one side.

When Charley Mason came over to see Bert one day he found his friend busy in the barn with some barrel staves, old skate straps, a hammer, nails and other things.

"What are you doing?" asked Charley.

"Making snowshoes," Bert answered. "I'm using barrel staves. They are long and broad, and if I can fasten them to my feet with straps I can walk along on top of the snow, and not sink in."

"I don't believe barrel staves will make very good snowshoes," Charley said.

"Just you wait," answered Bert.

He fastened the straps to the middle of the pieces of barrel, and then strapped the strips of wood to his shoes.

"Now watch me!" Bert cried.

Back of the barn was a field covered deep with snow. It had not been trampled down.

"I'm going to walk out there," Bert said.

He shuffled across the floor of the barn. He could only lift his feet up a little way, for if he raised them too far the barrel staves would have become criss-crossed and have tripped him. So Bert had to shuffle along just like a Chinese laundryman who wears those funny straw slippers without any heels.

Charley opened the back door of the barn for Bert, who stepped out into the snow. He shuffled along a little way, and did very well, for the broad, smooth pieces of wood under his feet did not sink down in the snow, which had a hard crust on top.

"See! What did I tell you?" cried Bert to Charley. "I'm walking on the snow all right!"

But just as he said that a queer thing happened. He came to a place where the shining sun had made the snow very soft. In spite of the barrel staves, first one of Bert's feet sank down and then the other. A funny look came over his face.

"What's the matter?" asked Charley, who was watching him.

"I—I'm stuck!" cried Bert. "I can't get my feet up! The staves are caught under the snow, and I can't move! Come and pull me out!"

CHAPTER XIX

THROUGH THE ICE

CHARLEY was laughing so hard at the queer look on Bert's face, and at the funny way in which Bert stood in the snow, that, at first, he did not make a move to go to his chum's help. Then Bert cried again:

"I am stuck I tell you, Charley! Come on and help me. I can't lift my feet."

"Can't you, really?" Charley asked.

"No. The front edges of the barrel staves have slipped under the snow and it's packed on them so I can't raise them."

"All right, I'll help you," said Charley, still laughing. He waded out to where Bert was stuck. Charley's feet sank down deep in the soft snow. "I ought to have a pair of those shoes myself," he said, floundering along.

"Well, don't stop to make them now," said Bert. "Help me first."

But even with Charley's help it was impossible to pull up Bert's feet with the queer wooden shoes on. They had got stuck sideways in the deep snow. Finally Charley said.

"Oh, take 'em off, Bert! Loosen the straps and then you can pull your feet free, and lift up the barrel staves afterward."

"I guess that is the only way," Bert agreed, and he did it. Once his feet were clear of the staves, it was easy enough to raise them up and then he could wade back to the barn, carrying the staves.

"I won't try to go on the soft snow again," he said as he sat down on a box and once more fastened the snowshoes to his feet.

"Do you mean to say you're going to try it again?" asked Charley.

"I surely am," answered Bert. "I'm not going to give up, just because I got stuck once. Why don't you make you a pair of these shoes? There are some more barrel staves, and I'll get you the straps."

"I believe I will," Charley said, and set to work at once. Then he and Bert walked together over the hard frozen snow. As long as they stayed on this, where there was a crust, they were all right. They did not go where the snow was soft, and so they got along very well.

Freddie saw what his brother and Charley were doing, and he cried out:

"I want a pair of snowshoes, too!"

"You're too little," Bert said. But later on he and Charley made Freddie a pair, cutting the long barrel staves in two pieces. But Freddie did not find it as easy as his brother had found it, and he tripped and fell down in the snow, so the older boys had to pick him up. Then the small twin gave up the use of snowshoes.

"I like riding down hill better," he said.

Winter had now set in, with all its cold and snow, around Lakeport, and there were many days of fine coasting. Flossie and Freddie stayed on the hill Bert had made for them in the yard, but Nan and Bert, with their friends, went to the big hill, and used the bob-sled.

Then came a thaw and the coasting was spoiled. There were puddles of water all about, and one day coming home from school

Freddie slipped and fell right into a puddle which was rather muddy.

"Oh, Freddie!" cried Flossie, who was walking with him. "Your clothes are all spoiled!"

"Well, I—I couldn't help it," Freddie said, looking down at the dripping mud and water. "I didn't see the slippery place."

"You must hurry home as soon as you can, and change into dry things, Freddie," said Nan, who was on the other side of the street with Ellen Moore and Nellie Parks. Nan had seen her little brother fall. "Run," Nan went on, "I'll hold your hand so you won't fall again."

Freddie gave his books to Flossie to carry, and he hurried on with Nan, running so he would be warmer and not take cold, for though the snow was melting it was still Winter.

As Nan and Freddie reached the house, they heard several persons talking in the parlor.

"Oh, there's company!" cried Nan. "They mustn't see you, Freddie, looking like this. I'll take you up the back stairs and change your clothes myself, or get Dinah to. Come on."

But just as Nan and Freddie were about to

slip past the parlor door Mrs. Bobbsey came out to see who had come in, and with her came a boy about Bert's age. At the sight of him Freddie cried:

"Why, it isn't company. It's cousin Harry!"

"Oh, Freddie! What happened to you?" his mother asked.

"I—I fell down in a puddle," said the little boy. "But I couldn't help it, Mother. Oh, Harry, I'm glad you've come!" Freddie went on. "We can slide down hill—— Oh, no, we can't either," he said quickly. "All the snow is melted. But Bert made a hill in our back yard and when it snows again we'll have lots of fun on it. Did Uncle Daniel and Aunt Sarah come?"

"Yes, we're here," said Aunt Sarah herself, coming to the door. "Oh, but mercy, child! What happened?"

"Fell in a mud puddle," answered Freddie. "Where's Uncle Dan?"

"In there, talking to daddy," replied Mrs. Bobbsey. "But don't stand here talking, Freddie. Cousin Harry will excuse you until you change your clothes."

"Of course," answered Harry. "Where's Bert?" he asked of Nan.

"Coming along with Charley Mason. They're just down the street. I hurried on with Freddie."

"I guess I'll go to meet him," said Harry. "I'll see you when I come back, Freddie, and be sure you're good and dry."

"I will," promised the little chap, as his mother led him upstairs. "How long can Cousin Harry stay, Mother?" Freddie asked.

"Oh, about a week I guess."

"I hope he can stay until there's more snow."

Uncle Daniel, with Aunt Sarah and Harry, had come from Meadow Brook to pay a visit in Lakeport, just as Cousin Dorothy had come from the seashore some time before.

A little later, when Freddie had on dry clothes, he and Bert, with Harry and Charley, went out in the barn to play. Nan had to go to the store for her mother.

Freddie's hope that snow would come soon was not to be gratified—at least right away. The weather remained warm for nearly a week,

and what little snow was left melted.   Bert and
Charley had no chance to show Harry how they
could walk on the barrel-stave shoes.   But
Harry noticed how they were made, and said
when he went back to Meadow Brook he was
going to make a pair for himself.

Then one night the weather suddenly turned
cold.   It was a cold "snap," as Mr. Bobbsey
said, and certainly there was "snap" to it, for
the cold made the boards of the house crack
and snap like a toy pistol.

"My, but it's cold!" exclaimed Nan, as she
came down to breakfast.

"Just what we want!" cried Bert.   "Eh,
Harry?"

"Sure.   This will make skating all right.   Do
you think the lake will be frozen over?"

"We can soon find out," Bert said.   "I'll telephone down to dad's office and ask.   One of
the men can look out of the window and tell.
If it is frozen we'll take our skates down and
have some fun."

"I didn't bring any skates," Harry said.

"I've some extra pairs," said Bert.   "I guess
one of 'em will fit you."

He called up his father's bookkeeper on the telephone, and word came back over the wire that Lake Metoka was frozen solidly, and that already some boys were out on it, gliding along.

"Hurrah!" cried Bert, when he heard this. "Talk about good luck! And to-day's Saturday, too!"

A pair of skates was found to fit Harry and the two larger boys, with Freddie trailing along behind, soon went down to the lake. They were well wrapped up to keep out the cold. Nan said she would come down later with Flossie.

"I have to practise my music first," said Nan.

Bert and Harry were good skaters, and Freddie did very well too, for his age. But he could cut none of the "fancy figures" as did his brother and cousin. Freddie was satisfied to glide around with some of the smaller boys he knew.

"Will you be all right, if Harry and I have a race down at the lower end of the lake?" asked Bert, after a bit.

"Course I will," said Freddie.

"Well, then we'll leave you for a little while. But don't go over near the point," warned Bert. "It isn't frozen so solidly there. The ice is thin and you may go through. Keep away from the point."

"I will," promised Freddie. The point was where some land curved out into the lake, making a sort of little cove, and as this was a sheltered place the ice had not frozen so thick there.

Bert and Harry raced away, to see who would first get to a certain point, while Freddie stayed with his little chums. Pretty soon, however, Freddie felt cold.

"I'm going in my father's office to get warm," he said to Johnnie Wilson who was with him. "Come on."

The two little chaps were soon in the warm office of the lumber yard. Freddie saw Tommy Todd come in, having been on an errand to the post-office for Mr. Bobbsey.

"Hello, Tommy!" called Freddie, who was warming his hands at the stove. "Why don't you go skating?"

"Haven't any skates," was the answer, and Tommy smiled. He was poor, and did not have any of the playthings other boys had, but for all that he was not cross or gloomy. "Besides, if I did have a pair I couldn't go. I have to work to-day," Tommy went on.

"Oh, I could let you have some time off to go skating, if you wanted to," said Mr. Bobbsey.

"Well, I would like it, if I had the skates," Tommy said. "But, as I haven't, I'll stay and run errands for you."

"You could take my skates, while I'm getting warm," Freddie said. "I guess I'll be quite a while getting warm, too, for it's awful cold out."

"Your skates are too small, I'm afraid," said Tommy.

"Bert has an extra pair. I heard him say so when he gave those to Harry," put in Freddie. "Couldn't Tommy take them, Daddy?"

"Why, yes, I think so. If you want to go up to the house after them I'll telephone Mrs. Bobbsey to have them ready for you," the lumber merchant said to his errand boy.

"Oh, yes, sir, I should like it! I haven't skated for a long time."

Mr. Bobbsey telephoned, and a little later Tommy was gliding about the frozen lake on a pair of Bert's skates, which, however, were quite good. Bert had laid them aside when he had been given a pair of shoe hockeys.

"Well, I'm warm enough now," said Freddie to Johnnie, after a bit. "Shall we go out and skate some more?"

Johnnie was willing and out they went. It seemed a little warmer now, for the sun was up higher. Many skaters were on the lake. All at once Freddie saw Tommy skating over toward the place which Bert had spoken of as not being safe.

"Tommy! Tommy!" cried Freddie. "Don't go there. The ice is too thin!"

But he was too late. Straight toward the point Tommy glided and the next minute there was a cracking of the ice and Tommy went down out of sight.

CHAPTER XX

"Oh, Tommy's in! Tommy's in!" cried Freddie, as he saw what had happened. "Oh, he'll be drowned!"

"Let's see if we can get him out!" shouted Johnnie.

"No, we mustn't go near that place. It's dangerous—Bert said so!" said Freddie. "I'll run and tell my father. He'll know what to do."

And this, really, was the wise thing to do, for such little boys as Freddie and Johnnie could not do much toward getting Tommy out of the cold water. Some other skaters, seeing what had happened, were gliding toward the big hole which had opened in the ice, and more boys or girls might have fallen in had not a man, who was skating near them, warned them away.

"Keep back!" shouted the man. "If you go too near, the ice will give way with you. I'll see if I can get him out."

By this time Tommy's head was to be seen above the water. He knew how to swim, but one cannot do much swimming in ice-cold water, and with skates on one's feet, besides wearing heavy clothing. Poor Tommy was in a sad plight.

"Help! Help!" he called.

"Yes, I'll help you as soon as I can," answered the man. "I must get a plank to put down on the ice, though, so it will bear my weight."

A plank on thin ice acts just as Bert's snow-shoes did on the snow, it holds a person up, keeping him from breaking through.

While the man was running toward the piles of lumber in Mr. Bobbsey's yard, which was on the edge of the lake, Freddie and Johnnie, not stopping to take off their skates, ran toward the office where Freddie's father was.

By this time the men in the lumber office, looking out on the lake, had seen that something was wrong. And they guessed what sort of accident it was.   Some of them ran out, and Mr. Bobbsey followed them.

"Oh, Daddy!" cried Freddie, when he saw his father.   "He's in!"

"Who?   Not Bert or Harry, I hope!"

"No, it's Tommy Todd—you know the boy——"

"Yes, yes!   I know him.   He went through the ice, did he?   Here, men, get a rope to throw to him.   The ice is too thin to go close enough to reach his hand.   We must pull him out with a rope."

There were ropes in the office, to be used in tying loads of lumber on the delivery wagons, and Mr. Bobbsey caught up a coil and ran toward the place where Tommy was struggling in the water.

By this time the man who had warned the other skaters away had found two planks.   He carried them as near to the edge of the hole through which Tommy had fallen as was safe. Then Mr. Bobbsey came with the rope.   He walked out on the planks and called to Tommy.

"Catch hold of the rope, Tommy, and we'll pull you out!" shouted Mr. Bobbsey.

He tossed one end of the rope to the boy in the water, but it fell short. Pulling it back to him Mr. Bobbsey tossed it again. This time a coil fell near Tommy's hand. He grasped it and then Mr. Bobbsey and the other man, who was Mr. Randall, pulled Tommy out on the solid ice. Poor Tommy could hardly breathe.

"We must get him to a warm place at once!" cried Mr. Bobbsey. "I'll carry him to my office. There's a roaring hot fire there, and if we wrap him well in blankets we may keep him from getting cold."

In his arms Mr. Bobbsey carried the dripping lad. Luckily Tommy had kept his lips closed when he fell into the water, and he knew enough not to breathe when his head was under, so he had not swallowed too much water. But he was wet through, and ice-cold.

Mr. Randall first warned the other boys and girls about going too near the hole, then he stuck one of the planks up near it, with a piece of rag on it as a danger signal.

Beside the warm fire in the lumber office Tommy was undressed and wrapped in warm blankets. One of the men made some hot cocoa, and when Tommy drank this he felt much better.

"But you can't put on your clothes for a long time—not until they are well dried," said Mr. Bobbsey. "I guess Bert has an extra suit that will fit you. I'll telephone to my wife and have her send it here."

Sam, who was Dinah's husband, came a little later with an old suit of Bert's, and Mrs. Bobbsey sent word that Tommy was to keep it, as Bert did not need it any longer.

"But it's a fine suit for me," said Tommy, when he was dressed in it. "I guess it was lucky I fell in the water—I got some nice clothes by it."

"But don't fall in again even for that," said Mr. Bobbsey with a laugh. "You may take cold yet."

But Tommy did not. One of Mr. Bobbsey's friends happened to stop at the office on business, and, having a closed automobile, he offered to take Tommy home, so the boy would not have to go out in the cold air after his unexpected bath in the lake.

Bert and Harry, on coming back after their

race to the lower end of the lake, were surprised to learn what had happened to Tommy. And when he had had enough of skating Bert said he would go and see if Tommy had reached home safely, and if Mrs. Todd needed anything.

Bert and Harry, who went with him, found Tommy sitting near the fire in the humble home near the city dumps.

"I'm glad I don't live here," said Harry, as he looked around before entering the house.

"I am too," added Bert. "It isn't very nice. I suppose when Tommy's father was alive they had things much nicer."

Tommy smiled at his two boy callers.

"This isn't working," he said. "And I ought to be at work, for it's Saturday and I do most of my errands then. But grandmother thought I ought to get warmed through before going out again."

"I guess that's right," said Bert. "How is your grandmother? Father told me to ask."

"She isn't very well," Tommy answered. "In fact, she had to go to bed after I came home. She says she feels sick."

"Maybe she ought to have a doctor," said Bert.

"Don't let her hear you say that," whispered Tommy. "She's in the next room, and she doesn't like to think of calling in a doctor. She says she hasn't any money to pay him."

"But that's not right," Bert began. "She ought to——"

Just then Harry nudged his cousin, and winked his eye in a way Bert understood. So Bert did not finish what he had started to say. Instead he remarked:

"Is there anything we can do for you, Tommy?"

"No, thank you, I guess not," answered the other. "I'm all right now, and I don't believe I'll take cold."

When Bert and Harry were outside and on their way home, Bert asked:

"What did you punch me for in there?"

"I didn't want you to talk so much about a doctor. I guess they haven't any money to pay one."

"No, I guess they haven't."

"But what's the matter with my paying for

one to make a visit?" asked Harry. "Dad gave
me some money to spend when I came on this
visit, and I have most of it left. You've been
doing all the treating. And you gave Tommy
that suit; so I want to pay for a doctor's visit."

"We'll ask mother about it," said Bert. "I
guess it would be better to have a doctor see
Mrs. Todd."

Mrs. Bobbsey said it was very kind of Harry
to think of using his pocket money to pay for
a doctor for the sick.

"But you will not need to," she said. "There
are physicians paid by the city to visit the poor.
But I think we will have our own Dr. Young
call and see her. The city physicians have
enough to do in the Winter when there is so
much illness. I'll send Dr. Young, and pay
him myself."

Afterward Dr. Young told Mrs. Bobbsey
that Mrs. Todd was not dangerously ill. She
needed a tonic, perhaps, and this he gave her.

"But what she needs, most of all," he said,
"is to get into a better house. It is not health-
ful down there. And she needs more and better food."

"Then I'll look after her," said Mrs. Bobbsey. "I belong to a club, the ladies of which are glad to help the poor. We will make Mrs. Todd our special case. I'll see what we can do about getting her into a better house, too. She is a very good woman and Mr. Bobbsey says he never had a better errand boy than Tommy."

Mrs. Bobbsey and the members of her club did many things for Mrs. Todd and Tommy. They planned to have them move into another house, but as the weather was very cold they decided that it was better for Mrs. Todd that she should wait a bit before making the change. Mrs. Bobbsey often sent good food to Tommy's grandmother. Sometimes Bert or Nan took the basket, and, when the weather was nice, Flossie and Freddie were allowed to go.

One Saturday afternoon about a week after the country visitors had gone home, when Dinah had finished baking bread, cake and pies, Mrs. Bobbsey said:

"I wish Mrs. Todd had some of these good things. But I haven't time to go down there to-day, and Bert and Nan are away."

"Let us go, Mother," begged Flossie. "Freddie and I can carry the basket easily."

"Well, I suppose you could," said Mrs. Bobbsey slowly. "It isn't very cold out to-day, though it looks as if it would snow. But perhaps it won't until you get back. You know the way to Mrs. Todd's now, and it isn't too far for you. But hurry back."

The little twins promised, and were soon on their way. They had often gone on long walks by themselves, for they knew their way fairly well about the city, and down toward Tommy's house there were few wagons or automobiles, so it was safe for them.

Carrying the basket of good things Flossie and Freddie were soon at the place where Mrs. Todd lived.

"You are good little ones to come so far to bring an old woman something to eat," said Mrs. Todd, with a smile, when she opened the door. "Come in and sit by the fire to get warm."

"We can't stay very long," said Flossie.

But she and Freddie stayed longer than they meant to, for Mrs. Todd knew many stories and she told the little twins two or three as they sat by the fire.

"Oh, it's snowing—snowing hard!" said Freddie suddenly, as he looked out of the window when Mrs. Todd had finished a story about a little red hen.

"Then we must hurry home," said Flossie.

They put on their wraps and overshoes and, bidding Mrs. Todd good-bye, off they went. But they had no sooner got outdoors than they found themselves in a bad storm. The wind was blowing hard, and the white flakes were swirling all around them.

"Why—why, I can hardly see!" cried Flossie. "It's just like a fog."

"And—and it's hard to breathe," said Freddie. "The wind blows right down my mouth."

"We could walk backwards and then it wouldn't," said Flossie, and they tried that for a while.

The children had been out in storms before, but they could not remember ever having been in one where the snow was so thick. As Flossie had said, she could hardly see because there were so many flakes coming down.

"Take hold of my hand, Freddie, and don't let go," said Flossie to her brother. "We don't want to get lost."

Along the street they walked as best they could, sometimes going backward so the wind would not blow in their faces so hard, and when they walked with their faces to the wind they held down their heads.

"Are we 'most home?" asked Flossie after a while.

"Well, I don't see our house," replied Freddie. "We've come far enough to be there, too."

They walked on a little farther and then Freddie stopped.

"What's the matter?" asked Flossie.

"I can't see any houses, or anything," answered her brother. "I—I guess we've come the wrong way, Flossie. I don't know where we are."

"Do you mean we—we're lost, Freddie?"

"I'm afraid so."

CHAPTER XXI

THE STRANGE MAN

THE two BOBBSEY twins stood in the snow-storm, looking at each other. Though they were both brave they were rather worried now, for they did not know which way to go to get home. If there had been no snow it would have been easy, but the white flakes were so thick that they could hardly see ten feet ahead of them.

"What are we going to do, Freddie?" Flossie asked.

"Well, I don't know," he answered. "I guess we'll just have to keep on walking until we come to a house, and then we can ask which way our home is. Maybe somebody in the house will take us home."

"But we can't see any houses. How can we ask?" said Flossie, and her voice was trembling.

Indeed, the storm was so thick that no houses were in sight. There might have been some near by, but the children could not see any.

Nor were any persons to be seen passing along the street. If there had been, one of them might easily have set the twins right. But the truth of it was that Flossie and Freddie had taken the wrong turn in coming out of Mrs. Todd's house, and instead of walking toward their home they had, in the confusion of the storm, walked right away from it. Every step they took put them farther and farther away from their own house.

And now, as they learned later, they were on the far edge of the city of Lakeport, beyond the dumps, on what was called the "meadows." In Summer this was a swamp, but with the ground frozen as it was it was safe to walk on it. But no houses were built on it, and there were only a few lonely paths across this meadow stretch.

In the Summer a few men cut a coarse kind of hay that grew on the meadows, but as hay-cutting is not done in Winter no one now had any reason for going to the meadows.

"Well, we mustn't stand still," said Flossie, after a bit.

"Why not?" asked Freddie. "Can't you stand still when you're tired?"

"Not in a snowstorm," Flossie went on with a shake of her head. "If you stand still or lie down you may go to sleep, and when you sleep in the snow you freeze to death. Don't you remember the story mother read to us?"

"Yes," answered Freddie. "But I don't feel sleepy now, so it's all right to stand still a minute while I think."

"What are you thinking about?" asked his sister.

"I'm trying to think which way to go. Do you know?"

Flossie looked all about her. It was snowing harder than ever. However, it was not very cold. Indeed, only that they were lost, the Bobbsey twins would have thought it great fun to be out in the storm.

They were well wrapped up, and they had on high rubbers, so they were not badly off except for being lost. That was not any fun, of course.

"Do you know where we are?" asked Freddie of his sister.

"No," she answered, "I don't. It doesn't look as if we were on any street at all. Look at the tall grass all around us."

Standing up through the snow was the tall meadow grass that had not been cut. Freddie looked at it.

"Oh, now I know where we are!" he cried. "We're down on the meadows. Bert brought me here once when he was looking for musk-rats. He didn't get any, but I remember how tall the grass grew. Now I know where we are."

"All right, then you can take me home," Flossie said. "We're not lost if you know where we are."

"But I don't know which way our house is," Freddie went on, "and I can't see to tell with all these flakes coming down. I'll have to wait until it stops."

"S'posin' it doesn't stop all night?" asked Flossie.

"Oh, I guess it will," said Freddie. "Anyhow, we know where we are. Let's walk on and maybe we'll get off the meadows and on to a street that leads to our house."

Flossie was glad to walk, as it was warmer than when standing still; and so she and Freddie went on. They did not know where they were going, and, as they found out afterward, they went farther and farther from their home and the city with every step.

"Oh, look!" suddenly cried Flossie.

"What is it?" asked her brother, stumbling over a little pile of snow as he hurried up beside his sister, who had gone on ahead of him. "Did you find the right path, Flossie? But then I don't believe you did. I don't believe anybody, not even Santa Claus himself, could find a path in this snow storm."

"Yes he could," insisted Flossie. "Santa Claus can do anything. He could come right down out of the sky now, in his reindeer sleigh, and take us home, if he wanted to."

"Well, then," said Freddie, shaking his head as a snowflake blew into his ear and melted there with a ticklish feeling, "I just wish he *would* come and take us home. I'm—I'm getting tired, Flossie."

"So'm I. But I did see something, Freddie," and the little girl pointed ahead through the drifting flakes. "It wasn't the path, though."

"What'd you see?" demanded Freddie, rubbing his eyes so he could see more clearly.

"That!" and Flossie pointed to a rounded mound of snow about half as high as her head. It was right in front of her and Freddie.

"Oh, it's a little snow house!" cried Freddie.

"That's what I thought it was," Flossie went on. "Some one must have been playing out here on the meadows, and made this little house. It's awful small, but maybe if we curl up and stick our legs under us, we can get inside out of the storm."

"Maybe we can!" cried Freddie. "Let's try."

The children walked around the pile of snow, looking for the hole, such as they always left when they built snow houses.

"The front door is closed," said Freddie. "I guess they shut it after them when they went away."

"Maybe they're inside now," remarked Flossie. "If we knocked maybe they would let us in. Only it will be awful crowded," and she sighed. She was very cold and tired, and was worried about being lost. It was no fun, and she would have been glad to go inside the little snow house, even though some one else were in it also.

"There's no place to knock," Freddie said, as he looked about on every side of the round pile of snow. "And there's no door-bell. The next time I make a snow house, Flossie, I'm going to put a front door-bell on it."

"That'll be nice," his sister said. "But, Freddie, never mind about the door-bell now. Let's get inside. I'm awful cold!"

"So'm I. And another snowflake just went into my ear. It makes me wiggle when it melts and runs down inside."

"I like to wiggle," Flossie said. "I'm going to open my ears real wide and maybe a snow-flake will get in mine. Does it feel funny?"

"Terribly funny. But you can't open your ears any wider than they are now, Flossie. They're wide open all the while—not like your eyes that you can open and shut part way."

"Maybe I can open my ears wider," Flossie said. "I'm going to try, anyhow."

She stood still in the snow, wrinkling her forehead and making funny "snoots" as Freddie called them, trying to widen her ears. But she gave it up finally.

"I guess I can't get a snowflake to tickle me," she said with a sigh.

"You can have the next one that goes into my ear," offered Freddie. "But they melt so soon and run down so fast that I don't see how I am going to get them out."

"Never mind," said Flossie. "I can get a snowflake in my ear when I get home. Just now let's see if we can't get inside this little house. If the door is frozen shut, maybe you can find a stick and poke it open. Look for a stick, Freddie."

"All right, I will," and Freddie began kicking away at the snow around his feet, hoping to turn up a stick. This he soon did.

"I've found one!" he cried. "Now we can get in and away from the storm. I'll make a hole in the snow house!"

With the stick, which was a piece of flat

board, Freddie began to toss and shovel aside the snow. The top part came off easily enough, for the flakes were light and fluffy. But underneath them there was a hard, frozen crust and this was not so easily broken and tossed aside. But finally Freddie had made quite a hole, and then he and Flossie saw something queer. For, instead of coming to the hollow inside of the snow house, the little boy and girl saw a mass of sticks, dried grass and dirt. Over this was the snow, and it was piled up round, like the queer houses the Eskimos make in the Arctic regions.

"Oh, look!" cried Flossie. "It isn't a snow house at all. It's just a pile of sticks."

"Maybe it's a stick house, with snow on the outside," Freddie said. "I'm going to dig a little deeper."

He did so, tossing aside the grass, sticks and dirt. Flossie was watching him, and suddenly the two children saw something moving down in the hole that Freddie had dug. Presently a furry nose was thrust out, and two bright, snapping eyes looked at them.

"Oh, see! What is it?" cried Flossie.

Freddie dropped his stick shovel, and stumbled back. Flossie went with him. The sharp, furry nose was thrust farther out, and then they could see that it was the head of some animal, looking at them from inside the snow-covered stick house.

"Some one lives there after all," whispered Flossie. "Is it a—a bear, Freddie? If it is, we'd better run."

"Bears don't live in houses like this," said her brother. "They sleep all winter in hollow logs."

"Well, what is it then?" Flossie questioned. "Will it come after us?"

But the little animal seemed satisfied to look out of the hole in its house to see who had done the mischief. Then it began pulling the sticks and grass back into place with its paws and jaws.

"Oh, I know what it is!" Freddie cried. "It's a muskrat. They live in these mounds on the meadows. Bert told me so. This one's house looked extra big because it was all covered with snow. There wouldn't be room for us inside there, Flossie."

"I'm glad of it," answered the little girl. "I wouldn't want to crawl in with a lot of rats."

"Muskrats are nice," Freddie said. "Bert told me so."

"Well, I don't like 'em!" declared Flossie. "Come on, Freddie. Let's get away from here. That muskrat might chase us for breaking in his house, though we didn't mean to do any harm. Come on, Freddie," and the two little ones went on once more.

The storm was growing worse, and it was getting dark now with the heavy clouds up above.

"Say, Freddie," said Flossie, after a bit, "I'm tired. Why don't we holler?"

"Hoiler?" asked Freddie, trying to turn his overcoat collar closer around his neck. "What do we want to holler for?"

"For help," answered Flossie. "Don't you know, in books and stories, every time people get lost they holler for help?"

"Oh, that's right," Freddie said. "I forgot about that. Well, we can holler."

The twins shouted as loudly as they could, but their voices were not very strong, and the wind was now blowing so hard that even if any one had been near at hand he could hardly have heard the little ones calling.

"Help! Help!" shouted Flossie and Freddie together several times.

They listened, but all they could hear was the howling of the wind and the swishing of the snowflakes.

"Well, let's walk on some more," said Freddie, after a bit. "No use standing here."

"And it isn't much use walking on," returned Flossie; and her voice trembled. "We don't know where we're going."

Still she followed as Freddie trudged on.

"You walk behind me, Flossie," he said, "and that will keep some of the wind off you."

"Thank you, Freddie," was Flossie's answer. "But I'd rather walk by the side of you. You —you can hold my hand better then."

Hand in hand the twins went on. The wind seemed to blow all ways at once, and always in the faces of the tots. All at once, as Freddie made a stop to get his breath, he gave a shout.

"What's the matter?" asked Flossie. "Do you see something?"

"Yes, I guess it's a house," Freddie answered. "Look!"

He pointed to something that loomed up black in the midst of the cloud of snowflakes.

"I guess we'll be all right now," Flossie said. "We'll go in there and ask our way home."

But when they reached the black object they found that it was only an old shed which had been used to store some meadow hay. The door of the shed was shut, but Freddie tried to open it.

"We can go in there to get warm," he said, "if I can open it."

"I'll help you," said Flossie.

The two were struggling with the latch of the door when they saw some black object coming toward them out of the storm.

"Oh, maybe it's a cow," said Flossie.

"It's a man," cried Freddie, and so it proved. A tall, nice-looking man, his black beard white with snow, walked toward the children.

"Well, well!" he cried. "What does this mean? Such little tots out in this storm!"

"We're lost!" said Flossie.

The strange man laughed.

"Lost? So am I!" he cried. "It isn't the first time, either. I've been lost a whole lot worse than this. Now, as we're lost together, we'll see if we can't get found together. Here, we'll go in out of the storm a minute and you can tell me about yourselves."

With one pull of his strong arms he opened the shed door and went inside with Flossie and Freddie.

CHAPTER XXII

HAPPY DAYS

"THIS is better," said the man, as he closed the door to keep out the wind and snow. "This isn't exactly a warm house, but it will do until we get our breath. Now tell me how you came to be lost."

"We were out taking some things to a poor lady," said Freddie, "and she told us some nice stories."

'One was about a little red hen," put in Flossie.

"Yes," went on Freddie. "And when we saw it was snowing we came out in a hurry and took the wrong turn, I guess. We couldn't see any houses, and we hollered and nobody heard us, and then I saw this meadow grass and I knew where we were."

"So this is the meadows?" asked the strange man.

228

"Yes, sir, this is the meadows," said Freddy.

"We know we're on the meadows but we don't know where our house is," said Flossie. "We live in Lakeport, and we're the Bobbsey twins."

"The Bobbsey twins; eh?" returned the man. "Well, that's a nice name, I'm sure."

"And there are two more twins at home," went on Freddie. "They are Nan and Bert, and they're older than we are."

"They aren't lost," explained Flossie, carefully.

"I'm glad of that," the man said. "And I don't believe you'll be lost much longer."

"Do you know where our house is?" asked Freddie.

"No, not exactly," the man answered.

"Didn't you say you were lost, too?" asked Flossie.

"Yes, I did, little girl. I was lost. But now that you have told me where I am, I think I am found. And I think, too, that I can help you find your home. So you live in Lakeport. That's where I'm going."

"How did you come to get out on these meadows?" asked Freddie.

"Well, this is how it happened," the man said. "I was on my way to Lakeport, but, by mistake, I got off the train at Belleville. That's the station just below here. I did not want to wait for the next train so I hired a man with an automobile to take me on to Lakeport. But about a mile from here one of the tires of the automobile burst so the man could not take me any farther. Then I said I'd walk, as I thought I knew the road. I used to live in Lakeport about five years ago. I started off, but the storm came up, and I lost my way. The first I knew I found myself out in this big field which you say is the meadows."

"That's what they call it," Freddie said.

"Well then, now I know where I am and I know what to do. Do you think you can walk along with me?"

"Oh, we're not tired now," said Freddie. "We've had a nice rest in here. But do you know the way to our house?"

"I know the way to Lakeport. I had forgotten about these meadows. You see it was a good many years ago and I did not live in Lakeport long before I went away. But now I know where I am. When I lived in your city I used to come out here to hunt muskrats. If I am not mistaken this shed is near a path that leads to a road by which we can get to a trolley car. I don't know whether or not the trolleys are running, but maybe we can find an automobile."

"If you could find a telephone and telephone to my father's lumber yard office he would come in his automobile to get us," said Flossie.

"Well, perhaps I can do that," the man said. "Come along now, we'll start."

Out into the storm again went the Bobbsey twins. It was snowing as hard as ever, but they were not afraid now, for they each had hold of the man's hands, and they felt sure he would get them safely home.

"Are you all right now?" asked the man, as he walked along in the snow, kicking away the flakes in a cloud such as a plow might throw on either side.

"Yes, we're all right now," Freddie said. "But we'll be righter when we get home."

"So mamma won't worry," added Flossie. "Mothers worry when their children are lost."

"That's too bad," said the man. "It isn't good for mothers to worry. But I'll get you home as soon as I can. You two youngsters have had quite a time of it, but I am glad to see you are brave and did not cry."

"Flossie's got some tears on her face," reported Freddie, looking over at his sister.

"I have not!" cried Flossie. "Those are melted snowflakes. I wanted to get some in my ear, so they'd make a funny, tickly feeling," she went on, "but there wouldn't any fall in. Some sat on my cheeks, though, and melted, and it's those what you see, Freddie Bobbsey, and not tears at all! I hardly ever cry, so there!"

"You cried when I busted your doll," Freddie said.

"Well, that was a good while ago," Flossie insisted, "and I was only a little girl. I hardly ever cry since I've growed up."

"No, I guess that's right," Freddie said. "She's 'bout as brave as me," he went on to the man.

"I'm sure she is, and I'm glad to hear that. You are both brave little tots, and I'm glad I found you. Whew!" he exclaimed, as the wind blew a cloud of snowflakes into his face, "this storm is getting worse. I'll have some melted-snow tears on my own cheeks, I think."

The strays kept on through the drifting snow, and, all the while, it was getting harder and harder for Flossie and Freddie to walk. The piles of snow were up to their knees in some places, and though the man easily forced his way through them, because he was big and strong, it was not so easy for the little Bobbsey twins to do so.

Pretty soon they came again to the rounded pile of snow that the two tots had mistaken for a little house. The white flakes had covered the hole Freddie had made with his stick.

"Let's stop and see if the muskrat is home yet," proposed the little boy.

"What muskrat?" asked the man.

"The one that lives in here. I started to dig in so Flossie and I could get out of the storm, and the muskrat put his head out and looked at us. I guess he was surprised."

"We were surprised, too," said Flossie. "At first I thought it was a little bear."

"Ha! Ha!" laughed the man. "And so you dug into a muskrat's meadow-house to get out of the storm? Well, that was a good idea, but I guess if you had gone in the muskrats would have run out. But it was a good thing you found the shed, and I'm glad I also found it. We will soon be home, I hope."

They lingered a moment, as Freddie wished to see if the muskrat would come out; but the creature was, very likely, away down deep in his house of sticks and mud, eating the sweet, tender roots of the plants he had stored away before Winter set in.

Once more the man led the Bobbsey twins onward.

Pretty soon Flossie began to lag behind. Her little feet went more and more slowly through the piles of snow, and once she choked back a sob. She wanted to cry, but she had said she was brave and scarcely ever shed tears, and she was not going to do it now. Still, she was so tired and cold and altogether miserable that she did not know what to do. Freddie, too, was hardly able to keep on, but he would not give up.

At last, however, the man looked down at the two little ones, and he noticed that they were really too tired to go farther. He stopped and said:

"Come! this will never do. I must carry you a bit to rest your legs. Wouldn't you like that?"

"Yes, I would," answered Flossie. "But you can't carry both of us; can you?"

"Well, I can try," said the man. "Let me think a minute, though. I think I will strap one of you on my back with my belt, and take the other in my arms in front. That will be the best way."

"Oh, I want to ride on your back!" cried Flossie.

"No, little girl, I think it will be best for your brother to do that. I will carry you in my arms in front. That will rest you both."

The man had a wide, big belt around his waist, and, taking this off, he put it over his shoulders, buckling it so that there was a loop hanging down his back. He put Freddie in this loop, astride, so the little boy could clasp his arms around the man's neck. Then, telling him to hold on tightly, and picking Flossie up in his arms, the man started off once more through the snow.

"This is fun!" cried Freddie, as he nestled his head down on the man's neck, keeping the snowflakes out of his eyes.

"I like it, too," Flossie said, cuddling up in the man's strong arms.

"Are we too heavy for you?" asked Freddie. "'Cause if we are you only need to carry us a little way, until we're rested, and then we can walk."

"But I'm not rested yet," Flossie said quickly. She liked to be carried this way. It made her think of the time when her father used to carry her when she was a little tot.

"Don't be afraid. I can carry you for some time yet," the man said with a laugh, as he walked on through the drifts.

"You can put me down now, if you like," Freddie said, after a bit. "I'm kinder cold and if I walk I'll be warmer."

"Well, perhaps you will," the man replied.

"And I can walk, too," added Flossie. "My legs are all right now."

"I don't believe you will have to walk much farther," went on the man. "I think the path is near here, and then it will be easier for you."

The man soon found the path, though it was not easy to see, and, walking along that, they came to a road. A little later the Bobbsey twins and the man heard a bell ringing.

"That's a trolley-car!" cried the man. "Now we're all right."

And so they were. The trolley was one that ran between Belleville and Lakeport, and a little later the two children and the kind man were sitting in the warm electric car, speeding toward their home.

"I think I'd better get out at the nearest telephone, to let your folks know you are all right," the man said. "They will be worrying, and if we can't get another car we may find an automobile."

The car conductor knew where there was a telephone in a drug store that they passed a little later, and the man called up Mr. Bobbsey at the lumber office.

Mr. Bobbsey and the strange man talked a while over the telephone, and then the man, coming back to where the twins were just finishing their glasses of hot chocolate which he had bought for them, said:

"Your father is going to send the automobile for you, so we will stay here until it comes. I told him where we were."

"Was he worried?" asked Flossie.

"Yes, very much," the man answered. "Bert, your brother, went out to look for you but could not find you, and your father was just about to start out."

"Well, we're all right now," said Freddie, "and we thank you very much."

"Oh, that's all right," said the man, with a laugh. "In finding you I found myself, for I was lost, too."

In about half an hour Mr. Bobbsey's automobile came along, he himself being in it. He jumped out and hurried into the drug store.

"Flossie! Freddie!" he cried. "We were *so* worried about you! What happened?"

"Oh, we just got lost," said Freddie, calmly, "and this nice man found us."

"We found each other," said the stranger, with a smile, "and now that I have done all I can, I think I will go on my way. I came to Lakeport to find my mother and my son. They'll be surprised to see me for they think that I am dead."

"You don't say so!" cried Mr. Bobbsey. "Where does your mother live?"

"Somewhere in Lakeport. At least she and my son did the last I heard, though they may have moved. Perhaps you can direct me. My name is Henry Todd, and I am looking for a Mrs. James Todd and her grandson, Tommy Todd. I am a sea captain, and I was wrecked a number of years ago. It was on a lonely island and——"

"Say!" cried Freddie, so excited that he slipped right off the soda-water counter seat. "Say! Are you—are you Tommy Todd's father?"

"Yes, that's who I am," the man said. "But what do you know of Tommy?"

"Why, we'd been leaving a basket of things at his house—with Tommy's grandmother. Then we went out in the storm and got lost,"

Freddie cried in much excitement. "Oh, if you are Tommy's father we won't have to buy a ship and go off to the desert island looking for you, like Robinson Crusoe. Oh, how glad he'll be that you have come back!"

"And how glad I'll be when I see him and my mother!" cried Mr. Todd. "But you spoke of taking her some food. Is my mother poor, and in want?" he asked Mr. Bobbsey.

"She is poor, but not exactly in want. My wife and I and some friends have been looking after her. Your boy, Tommy, runs errands for me."

"Well, well! Tommy must be getting to be quite a boy now. And to think it was your children whom I found and who told me where I was, so none of us were lost. It is very strange! And can you tell me where my mother lives?"

"I can, and I'll take you there. It is not a very nice house, but we have a better one for her. Only she did not want to move in this cold weather."

"I can not thank you enough for being kind to my mother and my son," said Mr. Todd.

"But now I shall be able to look after them. I have plenty of money and they need want for nothing now."

In the automobile, going back to Lakeport through the storm, Mr. Todd told Mr. Bobbsey and Flossie and Freddie his story.

He had sailed away, just as Tommy Todd had said, some years before. The vessel of which he was captain was wrecked, and he and some other sailors got to an island where the natives were kind to them.

But for many years no other ship came that way. So Mr. Todd could not get home nor could he send any word, though he very much wanted to do so. In that time he found some pearls which were very valuable. So, when finally a ship did pass the island and take off the wrecked sailors, Mr. Todd had more money than he had when he started out. For the pearls were very valuable.

As soon as Mr. Todd reached a place where he could send word to his aged mother that he was alive and safe he did so. But in some manner the message was never received.

As soon as he had sent the message Mr. Todd

started out himself to get home. Finally, he reached the United States and took a train for Lakeport. But, as he had told Flossie and Freddie, he got off at the wrong station, and had come on in an automobile. Then came the accident to the tire and the storm, and the rest you know—how Mr. Todd and the Bobbsey twins met at the old shed on the meadows.

"Well, that is quite a wonderful story," said Mr. Bobbsey. "I'm sure your mother and son will be wild with joy to see you again. They have long thought you dead."

"I suppose so," said Mr. Todd. "The papers said my vessel was lost with all on board, and it did seem so when I could send no word."

"Only Tommy and I thought maybe you *might* be like Robinson Crusoe," said Freddie, "and we were going in a ship to look for you on the island, only I haven't money enough saved up in my bank."

"Bless your heart!" said Mr. Todd.

"I think this is what we will do," said Mr. Bobbsey. "We will stop at your mother's house, get her and Tommy, and bring you all to my house."

"Oh, that is too much trouble!" said Mr. Todd.

"No, not at all. I want you to have a happy time, and we shall be happy with you."

The automobile was stopped at the house by the dumps.

"I will go in first," said Mr. Bobbsey, "and tell your mother and boy that I have good news for them. If she were to see you too suddenly, your mother, who has not been well, might be taken ill again. I will prepare her for the good news."

You can imagine how happy Tommy and his grandmother were when they learned that Mr. Todd was alive. And when the ship-wrecked sailor entered the house Tommy fairly threw himself into his father's arms, while Mr. Todd kissed him and kissed his mother in turn. Oh! they were very happy.

"We found him!" cried Freddie. "And he found us! And now everybody found every-body else and nobody's lost!" Freddie was very much excited.

"Only I'm hungry," said Flossie.

The Todds and Mr. Bobbsey and the twins

were soon at the Bobbsey home, talking over what had happened. Mrs. Bobbsey became worried when Flossie and Freddie did not come home after the storm started, and she sent Bert to Mrs. Todd's house after them. But they had already left, and had become lost.

"Well, now Freddie and I won't have to get a ship and go looking for you," said Tommy, as he sat close to his father.

"No, indeed. All our troubles are over now."

And so they were. Mr. Todd had plenty of money to look after his mother and son and a few days later he rented a nice house into which they moved. He said he was never going to sea again. Then began happy days for those who had spent so many unhappy ones.

Tommy no longer had to run errands for Mr. Bobbsey, to get money to help support his grandmother. He often came to play with Bert, Nan, Flossie and Freddie, and the Bobbsey twins never grew tired of hearing Mr. Todd tell of how he was shipwrecked.

The Winter wore on. Christmas came. And what a happy one it was for the Todd family, as well as for the Bobbsey twins!

"We had as much fun at home this Winter as we did in the Summer at Meadow Brook," said Nan.

Winter or summer, these lively children manage to have a good time. Their next adventure will be called "The Bobbsey Twins in a Great City."

Now as they gathered in the living room Freddie said, "I'm glad we found Mr. Todd."

"And he found us," added Flossie.

Snap, the big dog, thumped his tail on the floor in front of the fire. Snoop, the black cat, purred in her sleep. Outside the snow was falling and Freddie cried:

"Now we can have more coasting!"

"And there'll be more skating, too," said Bert.

"But I'm not going to fall in again," said Tommy Todd.

And now, as every one is happy, we will say good-bye to the Bobbsey twins.

THE END